SYSTEMA PARADOXA

ACCOUNTS OF CRYPTOZOOLOGICAL IMPORT

VOLUME 26
THE LAST SUMMER
A TALE OF THE GLAWACKUS

AS ACCOUNTED BY JACOB JONES-GOLDSTEIN
ILLUSTRATED BY JW HARP

NEOPARADOXA

Pennsville, NJ

2025

PUBLISHED BY
NeoParadoxa
A division of eSpec Books
PO Box 242
Pennsville, NJ 08070
www.especbooks.com

ISBN: 978-1-965266-11-3
ISBN (ebook): 978-1-965266-12-0

All persons, places, and events in this book are fictitious, and any resemblance to actual persons, places, or events is purely coincidental.

Interior Design: Danielle McPhail
www.sidhenadaire.com

Cover Art: JW Harp
Cover Design: Mike and Danielle McPhail, McP Digital Graphics
Interior Illustration: JW Harp

Copyediting: Greg Schauer and John L. French

DEDICATION

To my wife, Jennie,
who is a werewolf at heart.

Chapter One

June 1993

"Someday I Suppose" by the Mighty Mighty Bosstones played on the cd player as Woodrow Wright leaned against his friend Shawn's Thunderbird. The song felt like a perfect match to the summer breeze cooling the sweat dripping down his neck. He nodded his head along to the music as he watched two cars race down "the Track," a closed-off stretch of road behind what was now his former high school.

He and a good chunk of the people gathered around had graduated three weeks ago. Suddenly being high school graduates hadn't changed the lack of things to do on a Friday night in Stamford, CT so they were all back here hanging out and killing time.

Woodrow had walked over after finishing up his shift at the A&P to meet his best friends, Shawn and Kevin. Despite being a new-minted graduate, Woodrow didn't have a car, or even a license, so he was still hoofing it most places. Kevin didn't have a car either, so they both relied on Shawn to drive them around just about every weekend night.

"Someday I Suppose" changed over to "Holy Smoke" as Kevin walked back over after taking a leak behind a nearby dumpster. "Where's Shawn?" he asked.

"He's over talking to Tim and Carla," Woodrow answered, waving noncommittally to a pod of people standing around a nearby Jeep.

"Didn't they break up again?" Kevin asked.

Woodrow shrugged, "I thought so, but it doesn't ever seem to take, so who knows."

Kevin leaned on the car next to Woodrow and made several exaggerated sniffs in his direction, "You kinda stink."

"Bite me," Woodrow responded, then lifted his arm and smelled his armpit. "Ugh, yeah, I kinda do." He had sweated more than he thought on the two-mile hike from the A&P. Walking over to the passenger side door, he opened it before leaning in and rustling around in the glove compartment, pulling out a small bottle of cologne. He unscrewed the top and poured some into his hands, then rubbed it on his neck and under his arms. After a couple of test sniffs, he went back over to Kevin, "How's that?"

"Now you smell like Shawn," Kevin responded sarcastically.

"Technically, I smell like Joop."

"The hell is Joop?"

Woodrow laughed. "No idea, but that's what was in the glove compartment."

Kevin smirked, "I still think it's funny that a guy who has had one date in four years keeps cologne in his glove compartment."

"How many dates have you had?" Woodrow retorted with a laugh.

"That's not relevant. I don't keep cologne in my car."

"You don't have a car."

Kevin said with a shrug. "I don't have any cologne either."

Woodrow shook his head, grinning, "Those two things probably explain the number of dates."

Kevin thought for a second, "Shawn has both, and he's only had the one, and frankly, it was with Patty, so it barely counts."

"True," Woodrow responded, "Maybe we just suck."

They both contemplated whether they just sucked or not as the song on the CD changed to "Illegal Left," and another set of cars took off in a relatively short drag race.

"Yo, Wood!" Shawn called as he walked up the track toward Kevin and Woodrow, "When did you get here?"

They greeted each other with a complicated, and not particularly well-coordinated handshake. "About twenty minutes ago."

"How was work?" Shawn asked.

"A lady yelled at me because I wouldn't let her return an open box of tissues because, as she put it, 'they don't pull out right,' so pretty typical for the rich-people grocery store."

Shawn raised his eyebrow, and Kevin cocked his head, trying to figure out how tissues could pull out wrong.

Woodrow, Kevin, and Shawn had been friends since sophomore year, and Mr. Cardinal's first-period English class. The three of them weren't particularly troublemakers, but they tended to feed off each other when they got rolling and had more than once been told to knock it off. They had been friends since.

He occasionally wondered what things would have been like if he'd sat anywhere else that first day instead of between Kevin and Shawn. It was something that had been on his mind a lot, with college looming in a couple of months. Shawn was heading to UConn in Northern Connecticut, Kevin was staying local, and he was going to Boston.

He hadn't shared his worries about separating. The guys hadn't said anything to him either, but he knew they both felt the same edge on nights like this. For Woodrow it was like a clock always ticking in the back of his mind. It lent a sense of almost desperation to every weekend. There weren't many carefree summer nights left before everything changed. Since graduation, they got together earlier, stayed out later, and didn't skip out on opportunities to do things. Not that there was much to do beyond hanging out.

"So, what do you guys want to do tonight?" Shawn asked.

"Are hookers and blow an option?" Kevin responded thoughtfully.

Woodrow punched him in the arm, the corner of his mouth lifting in a smirk. "I've got $25 bucks."

Kevin made a show of looking through his wallet. "Yeah, a bit light here too. What's everyone else doing?"

"Zeta and Don are both working," Woodrow responded.

Shawn shrugged. "Tim and Carla are fighting. All the band types are going to see Jurassic Park."

Woodrow shook his head. "I told my mom I'd go see it with her Sunday. Wanna just go to your place and play video games, Kevin?" This was their usual default since Kevin's mom always fed them, and he had a Super Nintendo.

"Bobby's having a sleepover, so no-go unless you want to hang around with a bunch of ten-year-olds..." Kevin answered helplessly.

Shawn made a face.

Woodrow thought for a few moments but didn't come up with anything. "We could just rent a movie and go to my place, I guess."

No one responded for a few seconds, resigning themselves to a largely boring night before Shawn offered, "We could go bother the Moonies..."

Chapter Two

"Hey Jealousy" by the Gin Blossoms blared out of the speakers as Woodrow, Kevin, and Shawn cruised up High Ridge Road, heading toward Pound Ridge, just over the border into New York. The windows were down, and the summer air smelled like honeysuckles and freedom.

Trespassing at the "Moonie" temple was a time-honored tradition among Stamford's wayward youth. There was a temple for the famous Unification Church in the woods over the border, a strange-looking building with a driveway so you could pull up close to it. Just about everyone they knew had a story about getting chased off the property, usually by men with guns that shot sand. None of them really knew much about the Unification Church other than claims that they were a cult. That was enough to spark all of their interest.

Bailing on the Track, they headed over to Burger King to grab something to eat and kill time until it was fully dark. They had discussed going up earlier, but Woodrow convinced them that it would be safer to wait.

After finishing up a round of bacon cheeseburgers and fries, they popped into the A&P to grab a dozen eggs for the night's amusement. As they exited the store, Woodrow shouted, "Shotgun!"

Kevin gave him a dirty look, but climbed through the passenger door into the back seat.

None of them said much as they cruised up the road, each lost in thought. Woodrow's gut fluttered and flipped. He told himself it was the fast food, but this was their first time doing this together. Shawn had come up once with another group of friends during freshman year, but he had been drunk and didn't remember much. Their friend Tim had given them directions before they left the Track, of course, he'd been a little lit at the time.

"I think the turn is coming up," Woodrow said, breaking the silence.

Shawn lowered the volume of the music and slowed down a little. "Naw, it's the next left."

The houses out this way were far apart and back from the road into the woods. Calling them houses was selling them short in Woodrow's mind as they were all three or four times as large as the blue-collar neighborhoods where he and the others lived.

"You'd think they could afford some streetlights," Kevin chimed in from the back seat.

"Here it is," Shawn said, mostly to himself, as he eased the brakes to make a sharp left onto a thickly wooded street. "Until I Fall Away" began to play and Woodrow's pulse quickened as they drew closer.

Driving down a dark, wooded road to trespass on a cult's property, with one of their least reliable friends being the only one who knew where they were, was enough to make Woodrow nervous. The invincibility of his youth was still firmly a part of him, but with college looming and the uncertainty of those changes, he could feel the sharp edges of mortality teasing around the perimeter.

"So what's the plan?" Woodrow asked.

Shawn thought for a second and said, "It's a long driveway. You can't see anything from the road. I say we drive up till we can see the temple and then do whatever. Throw rocks or something."

"We could throw that awful bottle of cologne in your glove compartment. That'll teach them to be in a cult." Kevin barked from the back seat, cutting the tension clean through.

"Hey, that stuff is nice!" Shawn said with mock hurt in his voice.

"Sure is. I tossed some on my pits earlier and Kevin hasn't complained I stink since."

"Wait, you what?" Shawn said with less mock and more real hurt in his voice.

Kevin whistled two sharp whistles from the back. It was an old habit to get people to shut up that drove everyone else nuts. They usually shut up, though Kevin had observed and kept on doing it. "That's the turn, isn't it?"

"Yeah, yeah," Shawn said and dropped his speed to a crawl.

"Kill the headlights," Woodrow said while he turned the music off.

The driveway was a single lane that disappeared into thick woods after about ten yards.

Shawn pulled the car in and crept up the narrow path. The trees on either side of the road left just enough room for a single vehicle, and the way they leaned over made it feel like a tunnel.

"Well, this is creepy as hell," Woodrow commented. Shawn grunted in agreement while trying to navigate the nearly constant twists and turns without light. Before long, they reached a straightaway that had more room on either side, just about enough for a car to pull over and let another car pass. The straight part lasted about ten yards before quickly turning back into spaghetti.

Eventually, they reached a stone fence with an archway over the road. A wooden sign hung from the arch, but with the headlights out, they couldn't read what it said. Up ahead, lights shown faintly through the trees, flickering through the gaps in the branches as they drove.

Finally, the trees thinned, and the road led to a small parking lot. Just beyond rose a huge building with a front made entirely of glass. His gut clenching, Woodrow fingered the carton of eggs, his grip a little firmer than was likely wise. That didn't look to like a temple or a church to him. More like an office building. Blocky and three or four stories tall. The shape made the rounded front doors stand out. There were some lights on, and several pickup trucks parked out front.

"Looks like folks are home," Shawn whispered.

The three of them sat there idling for what felt like twenty minutes, but was closer to two, before Kevin said, "Maybe this isn't a good idea. We should go before they notice us unless you wan…"

He was cut off by an ear-splitting, inhuman-sounding scream from somewhere behind them, back down the mile-long driveway.

"What the *hell* was *that*?" Woodrow yelled. The carton in his lap gave beneath his tightening grip.

"Nope, screw this," Shawn said, slammed the car into reverse, and hit the gas. The car jerked briefly and then took off backward down the driveway. As they pulled away, they could see people pouring out of the temple.

"Go, go, go!" Kevin and Woodrow said in almost unison as Shawn tried to navigate in reverse at speed without lights on.

"Watch the wall, the walllll, watch the wall!" Kevin yelped.

"I'm trying!" Shawn shouted. He swerved slightly as he accelerated. Woodrow's heart raced as Shawn narrowly missing the stone wall.

There was another of those horrifying screams, much closer.

"Jesus Christ!" Woodrow exclaimed.

Kevin shouted, "Yo, the straight part, you can turn around here."

Shawn executed the fastest three-point turn Woodrow had ever seen, pulling most of the way onto the ground next to the road and then back on the pavement.

As soon as they faced the right way on the road, he slammed his foot down on the gas. The tires squealed and then caught, sending them flying forward. They went ten feet into the first turn and slammed directly into someone or something that leapt onto the road in front of them.

"Oh SHIT!" Shawn exclaimed.

"What was that?" Woodrow yelled.

"Did we just kill a dude?" Kevin said in a voice that sounded way to calm to Woodrow.

"Shiiiiit," Shawn said, unbuckled his belt, and opened the door, the engine still running.

"What on earth are you doing?" The carton of eggs fell to the floor as Woodrow grabbed for his arm but Shawn was halfway out the car.

"I gotta check!"

"Goddammit," Woodrow unfastened his belt and opened his door. He remembered to pull the seat lever to let Kevin out of the back seat. They both clambered out and started toward where Shawn stood.

"Grab the flashlight from the glovebox," Shawn called over. Kevin pivoted and ducked back in to grab it.

"What did we hit?" Woodrow asked.

"I have no idea, but it ain't a person. Might be a dog." Shawn responded.

Woodrow sucked in a sharp breath. To his mind, hitting a dog was worse than hitting a person.

Kevin arrived with the flashlight, switched it on, and pointed it at the mound lying on the road in front of them.

Woodrow choked on a gasp, the other echoing his shock. *Something* lay in the road, but it wasn't a person or any animal Woodrow recognized.

It looked like something left over from Halloween. The size was right for a large dog, but everything else was all wrong. Its torso was thick, like a bear, and covered in dense black fur. Its limbs were in the wrong place; the arms were at the side of the torso, and the legs were at the end, like a person, but the legs were about the same length as the arms. The limbs ended in back feet that looked almost like those of a wolf, but the arms ended in what looked closer to hands. And claws… wicked, wicked long claws…

Woodrow gulped and looked away from the hands.

Despite the weird build, the head was the strangest thing of all. It had a mane, like a lion, and a flat face that looked like a cat but with a flatter nose and mouth.

The three of them stared at it in the dim beam of the flashlight.

"I don't think that's a dog," Kevin said quietly.

Woodrow just stood there in silence, the back of his brain freaking out, like he should know what lay before them, but he just couldn't focus past the shock.

"What do we do?" Shawn asked.

"I have no idea, but it's still breathing. Can we take it to a vet or something?" Kevin said.

"I don't know any vets that treat whatever the hell that is."

Somewhere behind them, up the driveway, the sound of trucks revved in the night.

Woodrow jumped, his head jerking in the direction of the noise. "We gotta go."

"Put it in the car. Johnny's home tomorrow. He's taking all those animal management courses. He'll know what it is."

"I dunno about thi…" Kevin started to say when Shawn bent down and started to pick it up.

The trucks roared closer.

"Help me," Shawn exclaimed. That broke their stupor, and Kevin grabbed the other end of the creature and helped Shawn lift it. Woodrow ran back to the car and popped the trunk, breath held against the creature's musky odor, like his pits earlier, only a hundred times worse. As fast as they could, they loaded the animal and jumped back in the car. As Woodrow buckled in, eggshell and goop seeping out of the carton beneath his feet, three sets of headlights reflected through the trees drawing closer.

"GO!" Woodrow yelled.

Shawn hit the gas and blasted down the road before the trucks could see them.

They didn't notice the light coming out of the trees and falling on the back of the car as they pulled away.

They definitely did not see the man standing on the edge of the woods writing down the license plate number in a little notebook before stepping back into the darkness as three trucks came around the bend.

<h1 style="text-align:center">Chapter Three</h1>

Shawn flew down the dark Connecticut road forty miles over the speed limit. In the distance behind them, they saw headlights on vehicles that were also driving well above the limit.

"I think they're chasing us." Kevin offered from the back.

Shawn barked out a laugh. "You *think*?"

Woodrow, normally the calming voice of the three, nearly screeched, "The Turn, the turn," while uselessly pointing ahead in the dark.

Shawn barely slowed the car, hitting the brake and turning the wheel just enough to blow past the stop sign and drift out onto High Ridge Road. Kevin, who had not thought to put on his seatbelt, slammed into the side of the interior and let out a loud "oomph." Shawn pushed the pedal and flew down the larger, straighter road.

The headlights following them reduce to pinpoints, then only darkness.

"I don't think they're following us anymore. You can probably slow down a bit. Not sure we wanna get pulled over just about now." Woodrow said more steadily than he felt.

Shawn, whose knuckles had turned white gripping the wheel, took a moment to react to Woodrow's words but eventually started to ease off the gas.

They drove in silence for another mile or so before Shawn asked, "You okay back there?"

"Yeah, but I don't think I'll forget my seatbelt for a while." Kevin answered, "So, uh, where are we going with that, uh, thing?"

"What the hell is it?" Woodrow asked and, after a moment, followed up with, "And why the hell did we bring it with us?"

Shawn glanced at Woodrow before turning back to the road. "Dude, I hit it with my car. I couldn't leave it to die or suffer."

"Okay, but now we have a *thing* in the trunk. It didn't look that hurt." Kevin responded. "But I bet you once it wakes up it will definitely be pissed.

"It's not like we could have waited around for the Moonies to find us," his voice was rising in volume, just on the edge of panic. "And there's no way I hit it hard enough to kill it, but it might have a busted leg or something."

"I guess," Kevin said in a tone that implied he had a different opinion on the matter. "Did it even have legs? Looked like it had nothing but arms."

Woodrow intervened before they started full-blown bickering. "Alright, so let's deal with the problem at hand… We've got something in the trunk, whatever it is, that may or may not be hurt. I don't think we can take it to a hospital, and I dunno any, like, all-night vets."

"Johnny is coming home tomorrow afternoon," Shawn said, "He's not a vet or anything, but he's taking all those animal courses. He might be able to help."

"So what do we do with it till then?" Woodrow asked, "I don't think my mom would be thrilled if I dropped a wounded, uh, dog in the guest room."

Kevin quickly jumped in. "My house is full of ten-year-olds, remember? So that's out. Also, that is *definitely* not a dog."

"It could be," Woodrow responded.

"It's absolutely not." Kevin retorted.

Shawn held up his hand, cutting them off. "We can put it in my pool shed. It's supposed to rain tomorrow, so no one is gonna be using the pool. There's a lock on the door. You guys can crash overnight, and in the morning we can decide what to do with it."

Woodrow considered Shawn's plan a moment before nodding. while Kevin grunted from the back seat.

"How about we stop and grab some food at the diner first? Suddenly, I'm starved. And I don't wanna go straight home if they're still following us." Kevin asked.

"YES." Shawn and Woodrow said in unison.

The Elm Street Diner was a safe haven. A place of comfort for all three of them, giving them a chance to wash up, catch their breath, and calm their frayed nerves. It was around ten o'clock, which was earlier than they usually showed up. For the younger crowd, it was a place for late-night hash and eggs or pot roast subs, all of which tasted better well past midnight. At ten, the older folk and families were still hanging about. It wasn't until the clock struck twelve that it became the sole provenance of delinquent youth.

The guys didn't talk much as they ate, each trying to think of the best course of action while keeping an eye on the trunk of Shawn's car. Normally, they would hang out for a while in their booth, but tonight, they finished up and left. Kevin and Woodrow called their parents from the payphone out front to let them know they would be staying at Shawn's house and then headed out.

Shawn's parents were not night owls and would have long since gone to bed, so when the guys got there, they moved as quiet as possible. The house was a two-story colonial revival with a garage added on the side. A small path led around the garage to the backyard. The shed was on the far side of the pool, right in front of the tree line.

The street was a typical suburban street with trees dividing the property from their neighbors. The trees weren't thick enough to call them woods, but they were enough to give the backyard some privacy from those on either side. The guy next door was a limo driver, and rarely got home before two or three AM, so they were confident no one would see them haul the thing to the shed.

"So, how do we want to do this?" Kevin asked, keeping his normally booming voice low.

Shawn waved toward the path around the garage. "Let's just carry it around and right to the shed."

"Yeah, I didn't think we were going through the living room. I meant, do you wanna get a sheet to cover it, or a baseball bat or something in case it wakes up?"

"I'm not sure we wanna look like we're carrying a corpse in case someone sees us." Woodrow chimed in.

"You think a dead dog-thing is better?" Kevin snapped.

Woodrow smirked. "No, but it's black, so less obvious what it is."

Shawn cut Woodrow off, "Shut up. Let's just carry it as it is. You guys grab it, and I'll get the gate and the shed door."

Kevin balked. "I don't wanna touch that thing again, my hands still stink."

"Oh Jesus Christ, fine, you get the gate, but let's go before my folks wake up."

Shawn went to open the trunk, but Kevin put a hand on it before he could. "What if it's awake?"

"Do you hear anything moving or banging around? Is there any yowling?" Shawn responded and whacked Kevin's hand off the trunk before flipping it open.

They all three flinched back and groaned at the stench that wafted out. Kevin gagged loudly.

"God DAMN, did it die?" Woodrow asked with a choked voice.

Shawn pulled his t-shirt up over his mouth and nose and leaned in. "Nope, it's still breathing, slowly though."

Woodrow quickly unbuttoned his work shirt, took it off, and wrapped it around his lower face. Shawn pulled his t-shirt all the way off and did the same.

"Ready?" Shawn asked.

"No," Woodrow responded but leaned in and secured his arms around the creature's haunches. Shawn lifted from the shoulders. They both groaned at the stench and the weight.

They left the trunk open as they carried the creature around the house. Kevin kept far ahead and opened the gate before jogging over with Shawn's keys to the shed. It took five tries before he found the right one, but he got it just in time. As soon as they arrived with the creature, he opened the door. They laid it down inside, and then they closed and locked the door.

"God, that thing stinks," Shawn said.

"I'm not sure you got enough Joop to cover up that smell." Kevin quipped.

"There probably isn't enough Joop in the world for that job," Shawn said as he closed the trunk, and they went inside.

Chapter Four

The night passed fitfully. None of them slept very well, Woodrow didn't know about the others, but he'd had nightmares all night. By morning, he had gotten enough rest to be functional but felt as if he was hungover. The others looked about the same.

Shawn's parents had already left to run errands, so they had the house to themselves, which felt like a blessing. They made coffee and ate cereal while they tried to figure out what to do next.

"Have you checked on it?" Kevin asked between bites of cereal.

Shawn nodded, "Yeah, I went and looked right after Mom and Dad went out. It's still breathing and still out."

"It look any different in the daylight?" Woodrow followed up.

Shawn shook his head. "Nope, still weird as hell. It's like someone crossed a monkey with a cat and a bear. Or something."

Kevin made a face. "What do you think it is?"

Shawn shrugged. "I couldn't even guess."

"I had an idea," Woodrow offered. "Why don't we go down to the library and see if we can find anything? You still have that old instant camera, right? Take a couple of pictures, and we'll bring them with us."

"I don't wanna leave the house with that thing out there. What if it starts making that noise again?" Shawn responded.

"You stay here then. Kevin and I'll go. We'll try and get back before Johnny gets here. You said that was around four?"

"Yeah," Shawn confirmed, "That sounds like a decent enough idea."

"Cool, I'll call my mom to pick up Kevin and me. We'll go back to my house because I gotta change, or I'm gonna throw up from the smell."

Kevin agreed, but before Woodrow could make a call, he asked, "Your dad has a hunting rifle, right, Shawn? You might wanna consider loading it. Just in case."

They all fell silent for a moment, thinking about the claws on the creature.

"Yeah, probably a good idea," Shawn answered reluctantly.

Woodrow called his mom for a ride while Shawn went out to the shed to take a few pictures. They sat and studied the pictures until she arrived.

"We'll be back around three," Woodrow said as he and Shawn exchanged an awkward handshake.

Woodrow went to the front passenger seat, moving his mother's bible and sermon notes to sit down. As they got in the car, his mother asked them, "Busy night?"

At Woodrow's house, he and Kevin cleaned up before taking a bus downtown to the main branch of the library. Kevin lived on the other side of the city and didn't bother heading home first. He borrowed some of Woodrow's clothes and then proceeded to complain about his taste for the entire bus trip.

Going to the downtown library always made Woodrow anxious. During his freshman year he'd worked on a report there. Afterward he walked over to the mall down the street and got mugged on the way. He lost $5 and gained a black eye. Whenever he came here, he could feel the echo of the incident in his gut.

"I'm not even really sure where to start," Woodrow said as they exited the bus in front of the library. It was an intimidating neo-classical building with giant granite pillars out front. The other branches were all friendlier, but they also didn't have the resources available here.

"Well, first thing I think would be looking through the papers the last few days to see if there's anything weird reported, like vandalism in North Stamford. Maybe we can get the last week or so of Advocates and whatever paper Pound Ridge has?" Kevin suggested.

"Does Pound Ridge have its own paper?"

"I'm sure all those rich folks at least have a newsletter." Kevin snarked.

"That seems like a good idea. Other things we could check are guidebooks, like wildlife and stuff. You'd think we'd recognize all the animals around here, but maybe not?"

Kevin nodded, "Sounds like a plan."

They talked to a librarian who gave them the previous week's issues of Stamford Advocates and Pound Ridge Reviews. They sat in the periodical room and looked through the papers from cover to cover. It wasn't exciting work and after forty-five minutes of reading, they were both fighting off the urge to fall asleep.

"Find anything?" Kevin asked. He was going through the Advocates, and Woodrow was looking through the Reviews.

"Nope. There is literally nothing interesting at all that happens in Pound Ridge, although..." he trailed off, looking at the classifieds section. "Huh."

"Huh, what?"

"Well, maybe nothing, maybe something, but look..." Woodrow laid his paper flat and pointed at a section. "This is all missing pets."

"Is that a lot?" Kevin questioned.

"Seems like a lot to me, but this is from Thursday. If you look at Monday's, there's none."

"That's kind of interesting." Kevin flipped to the classifieds in the paper he was looking at and found no listing for missing pets. "There's nothing in this one. Maybe the Advocate doesn't run 'em because it's a bigger paper, but that's still weird."

"The list is even longer in yesterday's edition."

"When is the first one?"

"There's two on Tuesday." He shuffled that paper aside and re-opened the Wednesday edition. "Five on Wednesday. Ten on Thursday and..." he paused to count the listings from Friday. "Fifteen on Friday."

"That seems like a clue," Kevin said with an air of pride, as if he'd figured it out himself.

Woodrow nodded. "Yeah, but I dunno what it really means. I guess it tells us that maybe this thing got to town Monday and hung out?"

"Yeah, maybe. You should check the previous weeks. See if there's anything from then. If they're listing missing pets in the paper, there's probably a day or two delay."

"Good point." Woodrow went over to the librarian's desk and requested the previous week's papers. As he waited, someone tapped him on the shoulder and said, "Hey Wood, what're you doing here?"

Woodrow spun around and saw Connie Reed, another person from his graduating class, "Oh hey, Connie, how are you? Didn't see you at the Track last night."

Connie and Woodrow weren't particularly close, but it was a small school. Everyone knew everyone else and ended up at the same parties.

"Yeah, I had some stuff to do, but I did end up going to see Jurassic Park with everyone."

"How was it?"

"Really good. The dinosaurs look real. It's nuts. So what're you doing here on a Saturday in the summer? Not like you've got homework anymore."

"Hah, yeah, I guess not." It occurred to him he didn't have the foggiest idea what to say. He hadn't thought that he needed a cover story in the library, but the truth was a little too weird for him to share with anyone. He hedged his bets. "Was looking for listings of missing pets or anything similar."

"Missing pets?" Connie questioned.

"Yeah, Kevin, Shawn, and I went up last night to, um, bother the Moonies," he paused, and she laughed.

"We did that a couple of weeks ago. Mike made it about halfway up that little driveway road before he got spooked, and we left."

Woodrow knew the 'we' in question was Mike, Connie, Lynn, Jodie, and Charlene. They were as generally inseparable as Kevin, Shawn, and he were. He had been close with Mike growing up, but over the last couple of years, they drifted apart a bit, having fallen into different cliques. They still hung out but not as much, and usually with larger groups. They were both going to the same college in the fall, though, and he wondered if they would get close again. Probably not. When friendships changed like that, they rarely changed back. He felt another wave of melancholy hit him.

He shook it off. "We made it all the way up to the building but got chased away by some trucks. We hit something on the way out, and I was worried we might have hit someone's dog."

"Oh no!" Connie yelped. "Oh, I hope not. Was it big?"

"Yeah, like German Shepherd size."

"Oh, phew. Melanie lives up in North Stamford, and her dog ran away, but it's a little thing."

"Ahhh, yeah, this was definitely big. Sorry to hear about Melanie's dog, though. Hope it turns up."

The conversation hit an awkward lull, and after a few beats, Connie said, "Well, I should get back to work. See you at Jodie's birthday party next week?"

Woodrow had completely forgotten about that party and hadn't decided if he was going to go. "Yeah, probably," he said. The librarian returned with the papers for him and nodded to Connie, who waved to Woodrow and headed out of the periodical room. He brought the papers back over to where Kevin sat.

"What's Connie doing here?" he asked.

Woodrow opened up one of the papers. "She works here."

"I thought she worked up at the Weed Hill branch."

"Moves around, I guess. You find anything else?"

Kevin shook his head. "Nope, nothing."

"She said Melanie's dog has been missing."

"I don't think Melanie's dog is coming back."

"Yeah, seems like that might be the case."

"Although if I was Melanie's dog, I'd have run away ages ago."

They laughed. Kevin and Melanie, who was a year younger than them, had never gotten along. Woodrow didn't much like her either but didn't hate her like Kevin. There was something about North Stamford kids and Cove kids, from the other side of the city, that never mixed well. Woodrow had grown up in Springdale, the midpoint, and got along with everyone.

They went through the papers again and didn't uncover anything else that seemed connected. The previous week had no missing pet listings, which meant that whatever this thing was, it hadn't been around long. They headed out of the periodical section and went to look at nature guides.

After about half an hour of going through them, they concluded that the Monkey-Cat-Bears were not among the native Connecticut fauna.

"Well, this was useless," Kevin said as he tossed *The Southern Connecticut Field Guide* onto the table where ten other nature books rested.

"Yeah, I guess this was kind of a long shot. Maybe we can look at different regions?"

"We could, but like, you were in Mrs. Brown's bio class same as I was. You remember anything about Monkey-Cat-Bears?"

Woodrow sighed. "Nope."

"Maybe the cult is doing weird experiments, and something got out." Kevin said, and then thought about it. "You don't think that could be true, do you? I mean, Moonies are known for group marriages, not so much genetic experiments, but..." he fell silent.

"That might be something we can check." Woodrow said.

"What, escaped mutants?"

"No, but we're looking at field guides for real animals. What if we looked at books about not-real ones?"

"Not real animals? What're you talking about?"

"Like, Bigfoot."

"You think we hit Bigfoot?" Kevin said incredulously.

Woodrow chuckled. "No, but maybe, like mythical animals like Bigfoot or The Loch Ness Monster," he was getting a little excited, "When I was a kid, I used to read these books by Daniel Cohen that were all about monsters and legends. I used to tell people I wanted to be a cryptozoologist when I grew up."

"You must have been a weird kid."

"Bite me. I used to love that stuff. Might be worth looking at that and seeing if any of 'em are supposed to be from around here."

"That does seem like a long shot."

"Any other ideas?"

"Nope. So I guess let's get some books. We got another three hours before we gotta be back at Shawn's."

CHAPTER FIVE

Shawn sat in his kitchen, staring out the back window at the shed behind his pool. He had absolutely no idea what to do. Kevin and Woodrow were trying to figure out what the thing was, and he was basically waiting for it to wake up and start screaming. He felt helpless, which was not a feeling he very much enjoyed.

He got up and paced around the room, a frown bowing his mouth as he tried to figure out what to tell his brother when he got home. The only real luck he had was that his brother was going to be there before his parents returned. Explaining any of this to his mom and dad was completely off the table unless he had no choice.

He had felt the weight of his parent's disappointment for months, ever since he chose to go to UConn in Storrs. His father was older and starting to have some health issues. They had wanted him to be close and help take care of him, but Shawn couldn't bear the idea of another year doing the same old things. He needed to get out and find something new. UConn wasn't really his ideal, but it was at least close enough that his parents could get used to the idea of him being gone, and maybe after that, he could transfer somewhere else, somewhere out of state.

Tossing a mutant dog thing and a story about him being reckless and breaking the law into that mix was not going to help matters.

Dwelling on all this as he paced shook the anxiety out of him and replaced it with an exasperated anger.

A knock at the door broke his thoughts.

Kevin and Woodrow would be another hour or two at least and his brother wouldn't knock, so he had no idea who that might be. He went to the front door and looked out one of the thin windows.

Standing on the step was a tall man who looked to be in his fifties. he had on well-worn jeans, beat-up-looking boots, and a plaid button-down shirt that made Shawn's skin itch thinking about wearing flannel in June. The man was wearing a camouflage hat that was the only thing that he had on that looked like it was purchased after 1985.

He saw Shawn peering out from the window and made a small wave with his hand that didn't come off as particularly friendly.

Shawn opened the door. "Hi, can I help you?"

The man spoke in a deep, raspy voice with an accent that Shawn associated with rural Connecticut and Massachusetts. "Hey, I'm looking for a Shawn," he paused and looked down at a small notebook he held in his hand, "Barks?"

"What's this about?" Shawn asked warily.

"That your car over there?" the man asked, waving his hand over toward Shawn's Thunderbird. He pronounced it 'Cah.'

"I'm gonna need to know what this is about before I answer anything. You don't look like a cop."

The man sighed. "I'm gonna assume you're Shawn, and that's your car. Were you up around the," he looked at his notebook again, "Wellspring Zen Monastery?"

"The what? I've never heard of it. I certainly wasn't anywhere near it last night unless it's down the block, and I don't know about it."

"So you confirm you are Shawn Barks?"

"Are you a cop?"

The man sighed again and reached into his pocket to pull out a wallet. He flipped it open and displayed a badge identifying him as a police detective from Glastonbury, Connecticut. "So I'll ask again, were you anywhere near the Wellspring Zen Monastery last night?"

"I wasn't anywhere near any monastery. I've never even been to Glastonbury."

"It ain't in Glastonbury. It's a little over the border into New York."

"Look, officer, that's my car, but I don't have a clue what you're talking about, and it seems to me that this isn't your jurisdiction, and neither would 'a little over the border' in New York be. And frankly, you don't look like a cop."

The man glared at him. "Don't sass me, kid, I'm not in the mood. I'm following a," he hesitated slightly, "case and got a report from this monastery about you trespassing up there."

Shawn's alarm bell started to go off. Something was very off here. There was no way the Moonies even saw his plate, never mind identifying the car and him so fast. That coupled with how this guy looked and acted, this all felt wrong to him..

"Officer, I wasn't anywhere but home last night after about eight o'clock. Now, if you don't mind, unless you're arresting me or got a warrant, I think I'm gonna close the door. You have yourself a good day."

He started to close the door, and the man put his boot in the way so he couldn't.

The man all but growled, "Listen up, kid. I've had a long day, and I'm not in the mood. You want to waste my time, fine. But I'll be back and," he looked around at the house, "I'm guessing your parents will be more interested in getting my questions answered."

He moved his boot, and Shawn was able to close the door. He locked it for good measure. The man turned and walked across the lawn back to an older-looking Jeep parked in front of the house. Once he was in the seat, he took a last glare up at the house and then drove away.

"What the hell is a gadzookas?" Kevin said incredulously.

"Glawackus," Woodrow replied.

They had returned all the flora and fauna guides and instead went and pulled every book they could find on mythological monsters and local legends. There were about two dozen books in the library about creatures similar to what they were looking for, and after about an hour, Woodrow found something that matched.

The book he found it in was a well-worn copy of *New England Myths, Legends, and Monsters* by Levi Nelson. The indicia indicated it had been published in 1971, and the card in it was brand new, making them think it had been checked out a lot over the years, and the old card had filled up.

"That looks like a manticore or something?" Kevin said, unconvinced.

"Yeah, a bit, but it's got a mane, and the paws look similar. The face is stubbier," he held the polaroid they had taken next to the picture, "But you can see the basic resemblance."

Kevin squinted. "Yeah, I guess, but the picture makes it look much bigger."

Woodrow shrugged. "I mean, it's a drawing. Read the text, though."

Kevin took the book and read it aloud in his best professor voice, "The Glawackus has been described as resembling a hybrid of several other animals, presenting aspects of great cats, dogs, and in some instances, bears. The specific aspects attributed to each vary from recorded account to recorded account. While the veracity of each description there is some consistency in the creature's size and temperament that are consistent."

"Yeah, see," Woodrow said, "That sounds exactly like what we've got in the shed."

"I dunno, man, this seems insane. The thing is weird-looking but terrifying? I dunno about that."

"Maybe we have a baby," Woodrow replied, and as soon as he said it, he knew that's what they had.

Kevin paled and his eyes kind of bugged out a little as if he two suddenly wondered where the mama was. "Well… shit."

Woodrow took the book back and read a bit more out loud, "The first widely documented accounts of the Glawackus were in 1939. Eyewitness reports began after numerous accounts of loud and unusual howling over a period of weeks and months. Police documents show investigations of missing pets. Several dogs that were used to attempt to track the Glawackus did not return," He cleared his throat, "Where the heck is Glastonbury?"

Kevin shrugged. "Outside of Hartford, I think."

"That's a ways away from here. Hey, this says there used to be hunts and stuff. I wonder if we could find something in the newspaper from back then."

"I'm not looking through eighty years of microfiche," Kevin opined.

"We probably don't have time for that. We told Shawn we'd be there by four, and it's just about three. We gotta get going. Lemme go copy this page, and we'll head out."

"Sounds good."

Woodrow walked off to the machine and stood there for a minute before coming back, "Hey, you got any dimes? It's ten cents a copy."

Kevin had some change, and they made a few copies. They decided to check out the book, as well as a few others, before heading out.

Once outside the library, they went over to the bus stop, and Woodrow felt his anxiety rising. Kevin seemed to notice and asked, "You really hate it down here, huh?"

"Yeah, I dunno, man, it still makes me nervous." He shrugged helplessly.

"Well, don't worry, I'm here to protect you." Kevin flexed his arms in an exaggerated muscle pose.

Woodrow laughed. "My hero."

"Just doing my job," Kevin said. He then followed that up, in a slightly more serious tone, "Shame I won't be there to protect you in Boston."

"Well I've never gotten mugged in Boston, so I'm guessing I'll be okay," Woodrow joked, not sure if Kevin was serious.

"Yeah, I'm sure. It's a nice city up there. Not as nice as all this, of course," he waved his hand around at downtown Stamford.

"Oh, yeah, the Jewel of southwest Connecticut," Woodrow scoffed.

"Don't you forget that when you're freezing your ass off up in those Boston winters."

The bus pulled up before Woodrow could respond. They got on and sat toward the back. They would have to transfer to another bus, but not for about ten minutes.

Woodrow wasn't sure what to make of Kevin's comments about Boston. Shawn and Woodrow were about as able to talk about their feelings to each other as two eighteen-year-old men could, but Kevin rarely did. Somehow, the conversation outside the bus made Woodrow feel a bit better, knowing that Kevin was thinking about the same stuff he was, at least when they weren't thinking about having accidentally run over a supposedly made-up monster and stuffed it into a pool shed.

Chapter Six

Shawn was highly agitated when Kevin and Woodrow returned.

"What's up?" Woodrow asked. "Where's Johnny?"

Shawn ignored the question. "Some guy stopped by asking about last night. Said he was a cop," he said as soon as they were inside.

"Hold up. A cop came by?" Kevin responded, shocked.

"He said he was a detective and showed me a badge, but I dunno. He was dressed like a hick, and he said he was Glastonbury PD, not down here."

Woodrow raised an eyebrow. "Wait, he said Glastonbury? Really?"

Shawn shrugged. "Yeah, why? I think that's upstate. It's certainly not in Pound Ridge."

Kevin and Woodrow looked at each other before Woodrow said, "We better show you what we found."

"Is it some kind of bear?"

"Well, not exactly." Woodrow handed Shawn the photocopies.

"What the hell is a Galwaycus?" Shawn said incredulously.

"Glawackus," Kevin corrected him, "It's a, uh, thing."

"Thanks, that's helpful," snarked Shawn.

Kevin pointed to the first paragraph in the book. "It's a supposedly made-up monster like Bigfoot or Nessie. Except, not so made up, it would seem."

"They're called cryptids," Woodrow said, giving Kevin a shove.

Shawn shook his head. "Nah, that's ridiculous. It's gotta be a bear or something."

Kevin held his hands up as if to say 'what are you gonna do.' "That's what I said, but you have to admit, the description in this book is pretty close to what's out in the shed." He cocked his head out toward the backyard. "Speaking of which, you check on it?"

Shawn nodded, "Yeah I went out about twenty minutes before you got here. It's breathing but still unconscious. I think we maybe concussed it or something."

"I guess that's possible," Woodrow said, "So the cop said he was from Glastonbury? But he was asking if you were up by the Moonies last night?"

"Yup, although he didn't call them the Moonies, he called it some kind of zen monastery."

Kevin cocked his head, "Really?"

"Yeah," Shawn responded, "I don't remember exactly what he said, but it definitely wasn't 'Moonies.'"

Woodrow laughed, "I wonder if all these years folks have been bothering some poor Buddhist monks or something."

They all chucked at the idea, breaking the tension in the room a little bit.

"Still," Kevin said, "It's still kind of weird that a cop from Glastonbury was asking you about trespassing in Pound Ridge."

"Not if he didn't care about the trespassing or the moon… er… monks," Woodrow replied.

"What do you mean?" Shawn asked.

"What if it's the thing he's interested in?"

Kevin and Shawn both started to say something, but Woodrow cut them off. "Think about it. The stuff we found about the Glawackus all said they came from Glastonbury. They're even named after the place. Maybe there's something more to that."

"What, like he was hunting it or something?" Kevin said, with the gears clearly turning in his head.

"I mean, why not?" Woodrow said animatedly, feeling a rush of excitement. "The book talked about organized hunts. What if they still do it and one got away?"

"And they just don't tell the rest of the world about some mythological monster?" Shawn asked, clearly not buying the idea.

"*Cryptid*, and I have no idea," Woodrow responded. "But it makes more sense than a random cop from East Nowhere Connecticut bothering you about driving up a driveway, doesn't it? Also, how did he find you?"

"That had occurred to me. There's no way any of those trucks saw my plates unless they had cameras all over the place, and even if they did, it was dark, and we didn't have our headlights on."

"Brake lights maybe," Kevin interjected, "But that's a stretch."

Woodrow nodded, "Not out of the realm of possibility, I guess. It's the only thing I can think of if it was the monks, but what if that was just incidental?"

"What do you mean?" Shawn asked.

"You said the dude was dressed like a hick, maybe he was hunting in the woods?" Woodrow paused and thought for a moment before continuing, "Yeah, that could make sense. So we heard it scream a couple of times, right? What if the guy shot it or something, chased it out of the woods to where we hit it? He might have seen the car while we were there."

They all went silent for a moment, considering the idea, before Shawn spoke up, "Why wouldn't he stop us right then and there?"

Woodrow thought for a second. "Well, the thing looks fast. Maybe he was too far behind it and only caught up as we were leaving. We weren't there long."

"I guess that's possible," Shawn said. "Seems kind of coincidental, though."

"What part of this doesn't?" Woodrow asked.

"Okay," Kevin stated, "Let's pretend that's what happened. What do we do next? Give him the thing? Did he leave a card or something?"

"Uhhhhh," Shawn stammered, "No."

Woodrow was surprised. "He didn't leave a way to get ahold of him?"

Shawn grinned, "I told him I wasn't there, and frankly, he was a complete dick. He might have been trying to intimidate me."

"So you were an asshole to him," Kevin chimed in.

Shawn flipped him the middle finger.

Kevin laughed. "So, that's a yes?"

"Maybe a little." Shawn chuckled, then grew more serious. "He said he'd be back and threatened to talk to my folks. I stonewalled him, saying I wasn't anywhere near the place. But also, he didn't feel right to me."

"What do you mean?" Kevin asked.

"He didn't feel like an actual cop. However, he did know my name. He must have gotten that from running the plate, right?"

"That would make sense, so either there's cameras, or he saw it and somehow got the info. And he's probably at least cop-adjacent," Kevin responded.

"There was still something off about the whole deal," Shawn insisted.

"When he comes back," Kevin asked, "Do we just give him the thing if he wants it and call it a day?"

Shawn shrugged, "I guess? I can't think of anything else here unless we wanna sell it to the Stamford Museum or something."

"I have a thought about that," Woodrow said, somewhat grimly. "That might be a bad idea."

"Why?" asked Shawn.

"Well, these things are a myth, right? A local legend." He paused for a second before continuing, "Then if they're real, how come nobody knows?"

"What do you mean?" Kevin asked.

"The book says the first sighting was in the '30s, then a bit in the '50s, and then nothing. But if they're real and this one is all the way down here with a guy chasing it, it would stand to reason that people know, and they're keeping them a secret, right?"

"I… guess?" Shawn said, clearly not fully following Woodrow's train of thought.

"How are they keeping them a secret?"

Kevin and Shawn thought for a second, and then Kevin nodded. "You're thinking they might do something to us since we know about it."

"Yeah," Woodrow replied.

"Oh," said Shawn, "Maybe we shouldn't tell Johnny about it."

"Well, shit," Kevin said.

They went as a group to check on the cryptid in the shed. They had the notion that the reason it was still out cold was that the cop who was possibly hunting it had hit it with some sort of tranquilizer.

"Well, it's still asleep, so that's good," Kevin said, "But Jesus does it still stink."

"Yeah," Shawn responded, wrinkling his face in disgust. "I don't really wanna roll it over to see if it's got a dart in it."

Woodrow backed up a few feet, took a deep breath, and held it. He then walked forward and got close to the cryptid to check. He let out the breath he was holding while rolling it over and grunted, "Man, it's heavy."

He didn't find any darts in the creature but did find some scabs and scars that appeared to have healed over. "It looks like it was in a fight. Or maybe a few of them."

"Would make sense if it's been eating pets from here to Glastonbury," Kevin said thoughtfully.

Woodrow got up and closed the shed door, replacing the lock.

"Ok, so now what?" Shawn asked.

Woodrow thought for a second and then said, "Have you checked the trunk? Dart might have fallen off in there."

"Yeah, maybe."

They went to the front of the house and popped the trunk of the Thunderbird. The stench was still there but not as bad. None of them felt the need to gag as they had upon opening the shed. Shawn rustled around and then got excited, "Hey, check it out!" He held up a thin dart with a long white body, about six inches long, and a tufted pink end. There was no needle attached.

"Bingo," Woodrow said, "It say anything on the side?"

"Nope, nothing." Shawn said after a few moments of inspection. "Seems kind of big, though. I wonder if it's, like, elephant-sized?"

"That thing is big, but not elephant big." Kevin said, "Although if you wanted to keep something unconscious for a long time, I guess you'd use a lot."

"Might have been using darts meant for its parent too." Woodrow offered.

Kevin and Shawn both looked at him, having not fully considered how big an adult would be if they were correct about this being a child.

Shawn shuddered. "That's not a real happy thought."

Kevin and Woodrow headed back inside. Shawn said he would join them in a minute and then took the dart over to the neighbors across the street and tossed it into their trash can before jogging back over and going inside.

"Well, I guess we gotta decide what we're gonna do," Woodrow said while washing his hands in the kitchen sink.

"You going to just keep washing your hands until all the hot water is gone?" Shawn asked.

Woodrow spit into the sink and kept on washing. "I can still taste the stench and feel it on my hands. I just basically molested a cryptid. I feel unclean."

Eventually, he stopped and sat down at the kitchen table with them. They were all silent for a minute. None of them had much experience with the police other than being run off for trespassing or just generally being teenagers in the streets. They had never gone hunting and had next to no experience with wild animals. They all felt out of their depth.

The phone rang and they all jumped like an explosion went off.

"Jesus!" Kevin uttered.

Shawn got up and answered the wall phone by the refrigerator. "Hello?" He followed that with his normal surly "Uh huh," and then a less surly "Okay," before saying, "See you then," and hanging up. Shawn was never much for long phone conversations.

"Who was that?" Woodrow asked.

"Johnny, he's gonna be late. He's meeting up with Ron and Ben before coming home since Mom and Dad are out till tonight."

"That's probably good," Kevin responded.

"Yeah, I guess," said Shawn, "I know we probably shouldn't include him, but he's got experience with animals."

"Well, until we know what we're gonna do, it seems smartest to just keep it to us," Woodrow said.

"We keep saying that and then not coming up with anything," Kevin offered, "not that I have any great ideas."

"Well, let's run through our options so far," Woodrow said. "We can call the cops and turn it over to them. We can wait for that detective guy to come back and give it to him. Or we can open the shed door and hope it leaves on its own."

"Or… we could call the news and tell them we captured a cryptid and then get famous!" Kevin suggested.

Shawn smirked. "And probably get called hoaxers and get kicked out of college before we even get there, while also maybe pissing off a cult or an evil detective."

"Okay, okay…" Kevin said, a little crestfallen. "I didn't say it was a perfect idea."

Shawn added, "Also, like, for all we know, this is a baby who is lost and scared, and we'd be signing it up for life as a science experience."

"You just feel guilty for hitting it with your car," Kevin snarked.

"So?" Shawn said defensively.

"It eats pets," Kevin said, not displaying much sympathy. "And kinda looks like it would eat us."

Shawn shrugged. "Still doesn't mean it's okay to hit it with my car when it's maybe just scared and alone."

"Hey, maybe that's it," Woodrow interjected, "What if we drove it up to Glastonbury and let it go up there? We don't get famous, but we maybe get it back to his family or at least its native area, and we get out of the way of the detective guy."

"We don't know if a single part of that is true, though," Kevin responded. "We're literally guessing at everything."

Shawn thought for a second before saying, "Yeah, but we aren't gonna get facts, and at least that gets it away from my house."

Kevin smirked again. "Seems kinda dubious. Although you said the cop was from Glastonbury, right?"

Shawn nodded.

They sat looking at each other for a long time, waiting for someone to come up with a better idea before Kevin said, "Hell with it, I got nothing. Can we stop at Duchess on the way? I'm starved."

"It's gotta be tomorrow," Kevin said adamantly.

Shawn frowned. "What if that thing wakes up and starts howling?"

Kevin shrugged. "Then the jig is up, and we deny everything."

Shawn gave a sarcastic laugh. "Just shrug and tell people it locked itself in my shed?"

"At that point, they'll be wondering what it is more than why it's in your shed, which," Kevin smirked, "I still think is a better plan than driving it home."

Woodrow chimed in, "It's gonna look really weird if Kevin and I don't report home at least once today. Kevin hasn't been home in like forty-eight hours. Even *his* mom is gonna start to wonder."

Kevin glared at Woodrow, "Even *my* mom?"

Woodrow raised his hands in a mea culpa gesture. "You know what I mean. She's usually easy going with you."

"Only when you guys are around," Kevin retorted.

"Whatever," Woodrow responded, "Point is, Shawn's family is gonna start showing up, and if we take off at," he glanced at his watch, "4:30 in the afternoon, we're not getting back anytime soon. It makes more sense to go up tomorrow."

Shawn sighed. "Okay, fine, but we gotta move it."

"Where?" Woodrow asked.

"Man, I don't know, but it can't be here another night. The shed is gonna stink forever, and with everyone home, someone is gonna notice. Plus, if that guy comes back, if it isn't here, he won't know where to find it. He doesn't have your names."

"That's a good point, but we still don't know where to put it," Woodrow responded.

Kevin quickly said, "Can't be my house. I got a ten-year-old brother, a dog, and a nosey mom."

"I don't have anything like a shed. I can't keep it in my house and…" Woodrow trailed off.

"What?" Shawn asked.

"I got an idea, but we need to go now, and we need to go by my place first."

CHAPTER SEVEN

After several nerve-wracking minutes wrapping the cryptid up in a sheet and carrying it to the Thunderbird, the three of them had driven to Woodrow's house and were now on the way to church.

Woodrow lived with his mother, who was the minister at a local Methodist church. He spent a lot of weekends mowing the lawn and helping maintain the buildings. It was a small, aging congregation, so there weren't a lot of able bodies for upkeep. All of that meant he had a key to both the church and the building next door that housed the church offices, and the event area dubbed "Fellowship Hall."

As they pulled up to the empty parking lot behind the buildings, Shawn asked, "Are you sure this is a good idea?"

Woodrow laughed. "Of course it isn't. It's a terrible idea, but it's the only one we had."

Kevin smirked. "You really don't think anyone will notice?"

"No one is gonna be in the Fellowship Hall basement tonight, of that I'm sure, and there isn't much in there, so if it wakes up, it can't do much damage."

"Just the furnace and plumbing," Kevin said.

"I didn't say *no* damage, but that's not the big problem."

Shawn looked at him. "What's the big problem?"

"Tomorrow's Sunday."

"Oh."

"Yeah, we gotta be out of here and on our way by, like, six."

Shawn and Kevin both groaned. Woodrow wasn't thrilled either. None of them were what anyone would even jokingly refer to as morning people.

"Welp, too late to turn back now," Shawn said resigned.

"We could just drop it off somewhere and wash our hands of the whole thing like smart people," Kevin suggested.

Shawn glared at him. Kevin raised his hands in a peace gesture.

The three of them exited the car. Woodrow went over and unlocked the basement door. He'd never liked the basement. He always found it extremely creepy. Not as creepy as his house basement, but close. He had to chuckle at the notion of storing a cryptid in a basement that already scared him.

Carefully, they carried it down and laid it by the wall opposite the door. It remained unconscious and didn't so much as whimper in its sleep.

Shawn drove Kevin and Woodrow to their respective houses with a plan to pick them up at 5:30 the next morning. After that, he headed home. When he got there, he saw his parents' car in the driveway. Parked across the street was a Jeep. The disheveled cop sat in it, watching Shawn's house. As soon as he parked, the cop got out and walked over. He was wearing the same worn-out pants and boots, as well as the same camouflage hat, although he had on a different flannel shirt.

"Ready to talk to me now, son?" he asked in his gravelly voice.

Shawn once again shuddered at the thought of wearing flannel in the June heat. "Buddy, we already talked. I have nothing else to say to you."

The man reached out and gave Shawn a quick shove. He stumbled backward a step before banging into the back of his Thunderbird.

"Hey, what the hell?" Shawn said angrily as he gathered himself and took a step toward the man.

The cop shoved him again and took a step forward, this time standing a foot away from Shawn, who was pinned against his car.

"Listen, I don't give a shit about you or the other punks in the car with you. I know you were out there last night, and I know you took something that belonged to me. I watched you do it, and I want to know where it is."

"Man, back the hell up, I don't know what you're talk..."

The cop gave him a quick smack across the face. "I'm not stupid. I can smell it from your trunk right now, and I could smell it in your shed." He reached into his pocket and pulled out a padlock with the shackle cut off and shoved it into Shawn's chest before dropping it, "Where is it?"

"Yo, everything okay over there, Shawn?" a voice called from Shawn's house. He turned to see his brother standing there at the front door, looking concerned.

Johnny was bigger and thicker than Shawn but still nowhere near as big as the cop. Shawn didn't want anyone else involved, so he waved his brother off. "Yeah, we're all good. I'll be in in a minute."

Johnny called out, "Okay, but just the same, I think I'm gonna have a smoke out here on the stoop."

The cop glared at Johnny, then turned back to Shawn and said quietly, "This isn't game time anymore, punk. When I come back if you don't give me what I'm looking for," he turned and looked at Johnny, "it's not going to be a fun time for anyone."

With that, he turned and stalked back to his jeep. He got in and drove away slowly, looking at Shawn until he sped up down the street.

"The hell was that about?" Johnny called from the stoop.

Shawn picked up the padlock. It was the one that had been on the shed. *We moved the thing just in time,* Shawn thought. He turned and walked over to his brother. "Aaron's cousin. He's upset at Aaron and wants me to talk to him."

Shawn worked part-time in a comic book shop. Aaron was the owner. Shawn wasn't sure if Aaron had any family at all, but he knew Johnny wouldn't know either. He didn't like lying to his brother, but everything about this situation felt off to him, and he didn't want anyone else involved.

Together, they went inside. His parents came home shortly after that and his brother didn't mention the incident, for which Shawn was glad. Happy as he was to see his brother, he excused himself early and went to bed.

Sleep didn't come easy. He tossed and turned all night, second-guessing every decision they were making. He thought Kevin was probably right, they should just dump the thing and wash their hands of it or turn it over to the cop, but he felt guilty about hitting it. Whatever it was, it just looked like some poor animal, and it was probably lost and scared. Every time he looked at it, he just saw a kid away from home, and he imagined himself feeling like that next year. He knew he could always come home. He wasn't sure the monster could without their help.

Kevin spent the evening with his family watching "The Mighty Ducks" for the fourth or fifth time. It was his little brother's current favorite movie, and he had to admit he enjoyed it too, but tonight, it made him feel down.

They used to watch movies as a family every Saturday night until he got to be a teenager and was out a lot on Saturday nights. That changed over the last year or so as Shawn and Woodrow started coming over, and they'd all watch a movie or two together. His parents loved them like adopted kids, which always made Kevin happy.

Hanging out that night without them and watching a movie with just his brother and parents again reminded him that the guys he considered brothers were going to be gone soon, and he'd be alone.

He tried not to dwell on it too much, knowing they had to do something incredibly stupid the next day, but sleep didn't come very easily for him.

Woodrow took one of the longest showers of his life when he got home. He tried three different soaps to get the stink of the cryptid off him and he could still smell it. He considered just tossing out the clothes he had been wearing, but he liked the T-shirt too much to get rid of it.

His mom was too wrapped up in her Saturday night ritual of writing a sermon and preparing for the service the next day to pay much attention to him or how he smelled, which he considered a godsend. She had made macaroni and cheese for dinner, so he shoveled a pound of it into his mouth while watching "A Fish Called Wanda" for the 300th time before going to bed.

The carb coma from the pasta overruled his myriad anxieties about the next day, and he was out like a light within moments of his head hitting the pillow.

Chapter Eight

It was still dark out when Shawn honked his horn out front of Kevin's house. He waited a minute and honked again.

Kevin finally emerged after the third honk. He was carrying a backpack and a baseball bat. He tossed both into the backseat of the Thunderbird and climbed in.

"We playing some baseball today?" Shawn asked.

"I hope not," Kevin answered groggily, "But I figure it can't hurt to have a bat with us in case it wakes up. Plus, I told my parents we were going up to Candlewood today, so mom packed me some snacks and my swimming gear in the bag."

Shawn laughed. "Maybe we'll go swimming on the way back. I've got a crowbar in the trunk. I guess it would be a good idea to keep that in the backseat once we get the thing."

Kevin agreed, and they headed out to pick up Woodrow, who lived closest to the church.

"You think any of this is a good idea?" Kevin asked.

"Not one piece of it," Shawn responded. "But I don't care. That cop came back last night and threatened me. Even if that thing is a baby werewolf or whatever the heck you called it, I don't want that guy getting his hands on it."

"He came back?" Kevin asked. He wasn't surprised, but that still worried him. The idea of some crazy monster hunter guy chasing them made this all seem so much worse to him.

"Yup. Smacked me, too. So if we get up there and see him, I may need to borrow your bat for a few minutes."

Kevin laughed, then sighed. "Shit, it's early."

The sun started to peek through the trees as they got to Woodrow's house. Woodrow was sitting on the curb, waiting for them.

He also had a bat.

The temperature was already threatening to move past hot and into uncomfortable as they pulled into the lot behind the church. No one had arrived yet, as Woodrow had predicted. Shawn backed the car up as close to the basement door as they could get, and they all got out. Kevin and Woodrow brought their bats with them.

"I don't think we're gonna need both bats, guys, if it's awake, we're already screwed," Shawn said.

Kevin and Woodrow looked at each other and then at the wooden bats they carried. "Good point," Woodrow said, and they tossed them into the backseat of the car.

They went over to the door and Woodrow hesitated before unlocking it. He pressed his hand and ear to the door to try and hear if anything was moving around. He couldn't hear anything, so he knocked twice and waited another minute.

"Just open it," Kevin said impatiently.

Woodrow glared at him before fumbling with the keys and putting the right one into the lock. He paused for another moment before turning it and opening the door. They all braced for the cryptid to come bolting out, but nothing happened. Woodrow peered in but couldn't see anything from the door. He shrugged and went in. Kevin and Shawn followed.

The cryptid was lying on the floor where they had left it, still mostly wrapped in the sheet. The stench wasn't as overpowering in the larger basement as it had been in the shed, but it was still present.

They all watched it for a while to make sure it wasn't playing possum but seemed still out.

Shawn went out to the car to make sure the lot was still empty and to unlock the trunk. Woodrow and Kevin wrapped it up and then lifted it, carrying it over to the small set of stairs and then out after Shawn gave the all-clear.

They were halfway to the car when Kevin, who was carrying the haunch-side, yelped and dropped his half. Unable to support the weight on his own Woodrow dropped his half and stumbled back.

"It moved," Kevin cried.

All three of them took a step back, but after a moment of watching, it remained as still as ever.

"I swear it moved," Kevin said.

"Maybe the leg twitched?" Woodrow suggested. "Dogs and cats kick in their sleep. No reason a Glawackus wouldn't."

"I guess," Kevin said, unconvinced.

As they stood there, a car drove past the entrance to the parking lot. It didn't stop, but the noise was enough to break them out of their stasis and quickly pick up the cryptid and hustle it into the trunk. Woodrow went and locked the basement door. His hand shook as he turned the key in the lock.

Once back in the car, Kevin asked, "Hey, can we stop by Foodbag? I'm hungry."

After a quick stop for donuts and Gatorade, they headed north on the Merritt Parkway. With the windows down and the warm air blowing through, it was almost possible to convince themselves they weren't transporting a cryptid and were just out for a day of fun. "Mr. Wendel" from Arrested Development came on the radio, and Shawn turned it up. They all yelled along with the opening scream and began to relax.

"State of Love and Trust" by Pearl Jam came on next. The song made Woodrow think of Saturdays the previous summer when they would drive up to Candlewood Lake for a day of swimming and grilling. There was a liquor store on the way that wasn't especially diligent about carding young people and they would stop and pick up a six pack of Heineken. None of them especially liked it, but it seemed like a more sophisticated choice than Budweiser. The beer and the grilling had made them feel like grownups, more formed than they really were. The last time they had been there, they were chased out by security for swimming out of bounds. They'd spent the whole ride home listening to the Singles Soundtrack and laughing.

"Remember how upset that guard was last year when he caught us swimming by the rocks?" Shawn asked.

Woodrow laughed at the shared memory. "We'll have to make a trip up there this summer."

"I've got my swimsuit if you wanna go today," Kevin chimed in.

"What? Why?" Woodrow asked, surprised.

I had to tell my mom something about why I was leaving at the ass-crack of dawn with you schmucks. Trip up to the lake made the most sense." Kevin explained.

"Huh, that's pretty smart," Woodrow responded. "I just told my mom I was gonna miss church."

"Yeah, but your mom actually trusts you for some reason," Kevin said sarcastically.

The cover of "Mrs. Robinson" by the Lemonheads came on, and Shawn said, "Oh hell yeah," and turned it way up.

None of them noticed a Jeep that was following them from a distance.

The trip from Stamford to Glastonbury wasn't particularly long. On a Sunday morning without much traffic, it took them about an hour and a half.

At roughly the halfway mark, when they changed from the Merritt Parkway to Route 91, Woodrow thought he felt something kick his seat. It only happened once, so he assumed he imagined it, right up until they were about a mile from merging onto Route Two and the cryptid howled.

Kurt Cobain was swearing that he didn't have a firearm on the radio when the ear-piercing sound burst through the car. Shawn very nearly swerved into a guardrail before steadying himself.

"Shiiiiiiiiiiiiit," Woodrow yelled from the backseat as he felt another kick. There was no doubt this time.

"I think it's awake," Shawn said shakily.

"And apparently hates Nirvana," Kevin said, turning the radio down. "What do we do? This is just about Glastonbury; do we just pull over and let it out?"

"We can't do that here. The center of town is just up ahead. I found a road that goes through the middle of the big woods on the other side. I'm heading there."

Another kick rattled Woodrow, and he heard a loud thump from inside the trunk. "Better drive fast."

The next twenty minutes were the longest of any of their lives. Shawn drove the speed limit to avoid getting pulled over as they went through the town of Glastonbury where many had once hunted the Glawackus with no success.

Woodrow had shifted fully to one side of the backseat and sat with his back to the side window, holding his bat at the ready. The

Thunderbird didn't have a lot of room in the backseat to swing a bat, but he was going to do his best if the cryptid burst through from the trunk.

It howled several more times, once at a red light. They were sure the people on the street or in other cars could hear it but hoped they would assume it was music playing or something else that wouldn't cause them to want to investigate further.

Once they were on the other side of town, Shawn turned off the main road and took a series of smaller roads where the houses were spaced further and further apart until they turned down a road that looked like it had been paved during World War One. The forest quickly took over, until they stopped seeing houses at all. They drove two miles down the road and found a pullout that looked like it might be the head of a hiking trail.

Shawn tucked in and stopped the car. They all jumped out. Woodrow nearly threw up with relief to be out of the car. Every nerve in his body felt like it fired when the cryptid howled again.

"Ok, we're here. Let's let it out," Kevin nearly shouted.

"How?" Shawn asked.

"What do you mean how?" Kevin responded.

"How do we do this, so it doesn't attack us? It sounds pretty pissed," Shawn responded.

Kevin swore.

"Kevin and I grab the bats and stand on either side of the trunk. Shawn, you pop it from the front seat, and hopefully, it jumps out and runs away."

There was a loud bang from the trunk as the cryptid tried to get out.

"Shit, okay, let's do it," Kevin said.

Kevin and Woodrow positioned themselves on either side, bats at the ready. Shawn opened the front door and grabbed the trunk release.

"On three," Shawn said and began to count down.

When he got to one, Woodrow, who was on the road-side of the car and could see down the way they came, saw the Jeep driving fast in their direction. He started to yell, "Wait." but it was too late.

As the latch on the trunk released, the muscular black shape inside burst out and landed five feet from the car just as the Jeep arrived on the scene and slammed its brakes.

The Glawackus turned and growled at the Thunderbird and, by proxy, Kevin and Woodrow. It leapt toward the car, and both bat-wielding, newly-minted high school graduates dove out of the way with high-pitched screams. The creature landed on top of the car, looked down at Shawn — who was frantically backpedaling away — with its cat-like eyes, howled, and bolted into the woods.

Everything went silent for a moment as Kevin and Woodrow got to their feet, eyes looking at the path the creature had broken through the underbrush.

Then they heard the loud cock of a shotgun, and a not-very-friendly voice said, "Well, this is a bit of a problem."

Chapter Nine

"You," — the man motioned toward Shawn — "pull the car into the turnout and park it. Don't try anything, or I'll shoot this one." He pointed his shotgun directly at Woodrow.

Woodrow put his hands up. "Hey, man, we don't mean any trouble. We brought your thing back. You can just let us go."

"No… you let it go," the man snarled, "Now get moving with the car. You," he said, nodding his head toward Kevin while keeping the gun on Woodrow. "Park my Jeep next to it. Again, do anything weird, and I won't hesitate to kill your friend."

He reached into his pocket and tossed his keys to Kevin, who grabbed them out of the air by reflex and stared at them in his hand.

"Now."

Kevin, Shawn, and Woodrow all shared a look and then they moved to do what the man told them to do. They parked the cars, so they looked as if people had stopped there to go on a hike.

"Now what?" Shawn asked once the cars were in place.

"Now, we're going to go for a little hike," the guy pointed the shotgun toward the woods just beyond the cars, the way the Glawackus had disappeared. "Let's go."

They hesitated but quickly realized they had no good options. As they pushed through the underbrush, they discovered a trailhead just out of view.

"Single file, please. We're gonna be on this trail a while." Shawn went first, with Kevin right behind, and Woodrow at the rear. The man stayed a few paces behind them, well out of reach of any attempt to grab the gun but close enough that he could easily hit Woodrow if they tried anything.

Woodrow was terrified. They had all been in stressful situations, but nothing like this. Even when he had gotten mugged, there were no weapons involved, just fists. The only thing he could think to do was try and make mental notes of landmarks so if they got away, they wouldn't get lost. That was no easy task as the woods were thick, and the trail was narrow and not very well used. They didn't have much trouble following it, but if they had to do it while running, it would be easy to get lost. He also noticed that none of the trees had markers or stuff carved into them, which made him think this wasn't an official trail and not as well used.

After about ten minutes of walking, which felt to them like hours, Shawn spoke up, "What are you planning here, buddy? People know where we are and will come looking."

"No, they don't," the man said with a bit of a laugh. "I've been watching you sneak around."

The notion that this man had been following them, and they hadn't noticed filled Woodrow with dread. The man was right. None of them had told anyone where they were going, other than Kevin's lie about Candlewood Lake, which was on the other side of the state.

"I'll bet you don't even know where you are, never mind anyone else," the man said, still chuckling with an awful amusement.

"Glastonbury," Kevin offered.

"You ain't in Glastonbury now, boy," the man snapped, cutting his laughter short in an instant. "You're in the Meshomasic Forest. Oldest state forest in New England. Bet you didn't know that?"

The three of them remained silent.

He continued, "Yeah, I didn't think so. You boys ain't much for planning, huh?"

"All we wanted to do was bring the thing back where it's from," Woodrow offered.

"Oh yeah? How'd that work out for you?"

"Why are you marching us into the woods at gunpoint? This doesn't make any sense." Shawn almost yelled.

The man's voice turned on a dime again from snarky to vicious. "Actions have consequences, boy. We'll discuss it when we get where we're going. But for now, shut the hell up. Next one of you that talks out of line is gonna finish our little hike with a limp."

They all stopped talking and focused on following the path.

Somewhere in the distance, there was a howl. None of them saw the man's grin at the sound.

They walked for an hour in silence. Each step took them deeper into the woods, and still no signs of a well-used trail. There was no trash lying around, no bike tracks, no graffiti, nothing to imply people had been this way in a long time other than the trail itself.

They went over hills and through gulleys. At one point, they went around a pond completely covered with algae. Woodrow instinctively wanted to toss a rock into it but fought the urge, knowing that on this particular hike it could get him killed.

They heard several more howls as they walked. It was hard to tell where the sound came from, but the volume was always about the same, which made Woodrow think the cryptid was keeping pace with them. Or there were more of them out there. A chill went through him.

This place felt wrong. Woodrow had spent a lot of time in the woods hiking and camping and firmly believed that forests had a feel. Some felt bright and cheerful. Some felt old and tired. He knew it might all be in his head, but he believed it just the same. This forest felt bad to him. He reasoned it might be the situation clouding his judgment, but that didn't change his perception.

Everything felt off. The air was too cool for a June day. The light was too dim. It looked like twilight, despite being around ten in the morning, with no clouds in the sky that he could see through the dense trees. The sound was all wrong, too. Or the lack of it. There was no rustling, very few bird sounds. All the usual forest noise seemed completely muted. Even their footsteps.

The place felt dead despite the greenery around them.

"What happened here?" Woodrow ventured to ask.

The man laughed. "Oh, you can sense it, eh? More perceptive than I would have guessed."

He didn't answer the question, but he did start whistling as they walked along. It took a second for Woodrow to recognize the song, it was "The Farmer in the Dell.'

Chapter Ten

The forest had gotten thick enough that it had begun to feel claustrophobic. Shawn, still in the lead, was having to push through branches and brush more and more as the trail got harder to see. Eventually, they pushed through and found themselves in a small clearing.

In the center stood a small cabin. Dingy and old, with wooden walls that were covered with moss, although the door and a tiny window looked sturdy. The gabled roof was also lousy with moss and had small plants growing out of it in spots but likewise seemed intact. Had they come across it in any other circumstance, they would have given it a wide berth, not because it seemed abandoned but because it *didn't*.

Around the outside, there were some signs of use, including an old cooler that looked relatively clean sitting by the door and an axe stuck in a stump by the side of the cabin.

On the far edge of the clearing away from the cabin was a larger stump, maybe three feet tall and almost three feet in width. Attached to it was a thick, heavy chain with a large metal collar at the end. All three of them stopped and stared at it as they took in the scene.

"Good news, we're here," the man said, "Why don't you step inside?"

Tired from the forced march and the fear of the man with the gun, they all looked at each other and then went inside with Woodrow now in the lead.

He stopped in the middle of the room, shifting nervously. The others huddled next to him as he glanced around the space. Clearly someone spent a fair amount of time here. A camp stove, books, and recent-looking magazines, as well as cans of food and bottles of water, and a couple of impressive-looking flashlights, were all sitting on a table and a chair next to a gas-powered space heater. There was a small, closed box next to the heater. On the other side of the cabin, against the wall, sat a cot and a sleeping bag, set up under a second window.

The walls and vaulted ceiling of the cabin looked much studier from the inside. The only thing adorning the walls were a few shelves that held a couple of beat-up-looking paperbacks and nothing else. The ceiling looked scratched up at a glance but solid.

"Go sit on the floor over there," the man said, waving his gun toward an empty stretch of wall.

After the long hike, they were glad to sit down, even if it was on a hard wooden floor.

The man pulled a chair out from next to the table and sat on it. He crossed his legs, rested the shotgun across his lap, and then grabbed a water bottle from the table. He opened it and took a long pull before making a very loud 'Ahhhhhhh,' and put the cap back on. They all watched the bottle thirstily.

Somewhere outside, there was another howl. It didn't sound very far away.

"Well, we've got some time to kill, so I guess I'll tell you a little story."

"You noticed it," the man said and nodded toward Woodrow. "Place don't feel quite right, does it?"

Woodrow didn't know quite what to say, "I don't, I mean… well, no, it doesn't."

Shawn said quietly, "The light is all wrong."

"And there's no birds," Kevin added.

"Well now, you're all smarter than I gave you credit for, or at least more observant," he continued. "You're right. It's rotten." His accent bled all over the last word, making it sound more like 'Rawwwten.'

"What does that mean?" Kevin asked.

"Some places are just bad. Something that other places have this place is just missing. Maybe a soul? They named it Meshomasic when it became a state park, which is Algonquin for 'Place of many snakes,' which I have always thought sounded about right."

Shawn asked, "Are there a lot of snakes?" It came out more sarcastic than he meant it. The man glared at him.

"Don't you start sassing me again just because it's story time," He took another swig of the water without offering them any, "Although there are. Rattlesnakes. Just about the only ones left in these parts. They made it illegal to kill em, too, which is dumb. Ain't nobody needs rattlesnakes slithering around," He turned his head and spat on the floor in the corner by the door.

Woodrow got the feeling the man didn't care for snakes. He didn't much like them either and, up until this moment, had no idea that Connecticut was home to rattlesnakes.

"Anyways, back in nineteen hundred something or other they made this place a state forest. Wasn't because they wanted to preserve it, but because lumberjacks kept disappearing whenever they tried to log here. Sure, they said publicly they wanted to save the trees, but really, they figured out it was evil and thought it would be best if everybody left it alone."

"You really believe this place is evil?" Shawn asked.

"You will too 'fore the night is over."

Ominous as that sounded, Woodrow was almost relieved to hear it because that meant this weirdo wasn't planning on killing them outright. He hoped, at least.

"So they made this place off-limits and left it alone. People ain't good at that, though, so people still came through, and a lot went missing. They dug a couple of quarries to mine some rocks, but that didn't last too long. They was pretty dumb if you ask me. You find a place like this, the last thing you wanna do is dig." He emphasized the last word like it was the most ridiculous thing anyone had ever heard before continuing, "You go down by them quarries now, and it might be a bright sunny day, but you won't be able to feel it. All you'll feel on your skin is cold. You'll keep looking over your shoulder because it'll feel like someone is watching you. And if you go swimming," he shuddered, "Well, never mind what, but it'll make you think twice about getting in the water again anytime soon. Later on, they even put in a site to fire goddamn missiles! I won't even tell you what all goes on where that used to be."

"Why're you trying to scare us?" Kevin asked.

"Ain't trying to scare you, boy. I'm telling you why you should be scared. Up to you if you got sense in your head," he said before continuing on, "Mistake they made was not burning this place to the ground. Instead, they let it fester and feed, and eventually, the shadows that live here got fat and bloated like ticks and burst open. When they burst open, they let some things that shouldn't be, be."

Shawn scowled. "Man, what on earth are you talking about?"

"Boy, you got a mouth on you," he said before pausing, "You ever see that movie Pet Sematary? 'Bout man who lets his kid get killed and buries him in a bad place, and he comes back?"

"Yeah, I've seen it," Shawn responded.

"Pretty sure that Stephen King was inspired by a visit here. It's like that. It's a place where you give it something, it gives you back something worse. People spent years feeding this place the overly curious, lumberjacks, and sometime in the '30s something got out."

"The Glawackus." Woodrow said.

"You really are the smart one," the man said, "Yup, the Glawackus, which is a pretty silly name you ask me, but no one ever did," he spit in the corner again.

"What are they?" asked Kevin.

"Don't rightly know. Way their eyes glow, I can tell you they ain't just mutant bears." He shook his head. "No, like everything else around here, they're unnatural."

"Their eyes glow?" Kevin asked, his own eye widening.

"Okay, it's a bad place filled with monsters, so why did you kidnap us at gunpoint and bring us here?" Shawn asked angrily.

The man grinned, "Well, well, that's the heart of the matter, ain't it?"

Chapter Eleven

"I'm gonna tell you all another lil story," the man began.

"The last one kind of sucked, not sure I need another one," Shawn snarked.

The man ran his finger down the barrel of his shotgun. "Tell you what, how about you and I go for a little walk."

"Huh?" Shawn said.

Kevin and Woodrow both started talking at once before the man shouted, "Shut up!" He then stood up and pointed the shotgun at Shawn. "Come on, let's go."

"You don't have to do anything, sir. We heard your story. You can just let us go, and we'll never mention any of this," Woodrow pleaded.

"Shut up, I said, and you, get moving."

"Please," Shawn began before the man cut him off.

"Too late for that, you little punk. Let's go."

Shawn got up and slowly walked to the door. The man waved him along, then turned back to Kevin and Woodrow and growled, "I hear either of you so much as sneeze while I'm gone, and we're gonna have problems."

Shawn went out the door, and the man followed him.

"What do we do," Kevin asked desperately, turning to Woodrow.

"Maybe there's something in here we can fight him with," Woodrow said before getting up as quietly as possible.

"You don't have to do this," Shawn begged.

"Not so goddamn sarcastic now, are you? Get over there," he pointed to the stump with the chain attached to it.

Shawn looked at the stump and then glanced at the axe in the other stump several paces away. The man saw him and laughed.

"Go ahead. Try for the axe… if you want to find out what life feels like without a foot. Get going."

He moved close and gave Shawn a shove in the back with the gun. Shawn walked over to where the man wanted him to go.

"Pick up the chain," the man ordered. Shawn looked at it at a complete loss.

"Go on, do it."

Shawn picked the chain up.

"Now, put the collar around your neck and clamp it shut."

"What the hell?" Shawn said, confused.

"Do it!" the man yelled.

Shawn flinched and then did as the man asked. It was heavy and cold, but it fit around his neck. It wasn't snug, but there was no way he could pull it off over his head.

"See? That wasn't so hard," the man said sarcastically, "Now, sit down and put your hands behind your back."

Shawn, who had begun to think the man didn't intend to kill him, got frightened again but did as the man asked.

The man tucked the shotgun under his arm and walked over to Shawn. "Lean your head back."

Shawn did so and saw the man pull a padlock out of his pocket. He snapped onto the latch on the collar. He then patted Shawn on the head. "Look at you, all that, and you didn't even piss yourself."

He took a sniff. "Or maybe you did? If that's cologne, you might wanna dial it back a bit."

Shawn was utterly confused at this point.

The man walked back over by the door and called out, "You two boys, come out here, slowly."

There was a long pause before the door opened. Kevin came first, and then Woodrow. They each very obviously had a hand behind their back.

The man laughed and pointed the shotgun at them. "Go ahead and drop the cans or whatever you think you have as a weapon."

There were two thuds as they each dropped a can of food they had grabbed from the table inside.

"I keep thinking you boys might be smart, and you keep proving to be dumb as hell," The man commented, "Now, take a look at your friend over there."

"What the hell?" Woodrow said loudly.

"Are you okay, Shawn?" Kevin asked nervously.

Shawn gave a little wave. "I'm okay."

"Now eyes on me, boys,"

All three turned and looked at the man.

"Pay attention," he said and held up a small key. He shook it a couple of times, then took it in his hand, reared his arm back, and threw the key into the woods. They all watched as it sailed into the trees. They did not hear the small key land.

"Hope you got a good memory, now get back into the cabin," the man said and then laughed. "Well, not you," he said to Shawn before following Kevin and Woodrow inside.

"Alright, let's try this again," he began after they were all seated again. Kevin and Woodrow were on the floor, and the man was once again on the chair with the shotgun across his lap. "Unless one of you has a problem with my stories like your friend?"

Kevin and Woodrow remained quiet.

"Ain't no one asked, but my name's Abner Johnson. My family has lived in this area since the 1700s. Johnsons fought in the Revolutionary War and just about everything since. Been here a long time, and it turns out we knew about the bad patch here since all the way back then."

He spit in that same corner. Woodrow wondered how many years of spit that corner had seen and tried not to shudder.

"Some of them originals back then were friendly with the Wangunk tribe, before they all got run off. When they went, they asked my family to do what they had done, which was keep an eye on the place and not let the things here stray too far. Ain't no way to clean a place like this, bad is bad, and it stays that way. Since you can't get rid of it, next best thing is contain it."

He took a long sip off his bottle of water. "So that's what we've done, down through the years. My family been passing down the job from every generation. Right on down to me. It ain't so bad once you get used to the idea, although you gotta be pretty damn careful. We lost a few here and there over the years. My brother included."

He stopped for a few seconds. Woodrow thought he looked wistful at the mention of his brother, but it was impossible to really tell.

"The problems come when things get out. You called 'em a Glawackus, so I'm assuming you read about the hunts and all ah that crap?" Abner asked.

It took Woodrow a second to realize he was waiting for a response. "Oh, yeah, back in the '30s and the '50s."

"Whole thing apparently got a bit crazy. People all over trying to catch one of those things. According to my grandfather, it was all because one got loose, and it took him a while to hunt the thing down. People saw it, and that was that. Of course, most people write alla that off as a hoax or hysteria. Sayin' it was a fishercat or something, which is pretty laughable. You ever see one of them things?" he asked.

Kevin and Woodrow shook their heads.

"They're about the size of a small dog. You saw the size of the little Glawackus, ain't no *small* dog," he chuckled, "Anyways, that was a situation like the one we find ourselves in today, wherein one of these things gets it in their head to go on a little walkabout, and my family gotta get 'em back before they're seen," he paused, and then said darkly, "It's when they get seen that we gotta problem. Because then people get curious."

He grinned at Kevin and Woodrow.

"At the very least, the big ones never stray very far. One of them decided it wanted to do a bit of traveling; wouldn't be much any of us could do."

"Why did you shoot it with a tranquilizer and not a bullet?" Kevin asked.

"The number of bullets it takes to bring even the little ones down is more'n a hunting rifle's worth, and I don't own a machine gun. Knocking 'em out seems to work, though it takes about the same amount of tranquilizer as an elephant would. And that's for the small ones."

"Okay," Woodrow said, "So what are you going to do with us? Why'd you chain Shawn up out there?"

Abner grinned again. Woodrow and Kevin were both beginning to dread that grin.

"I'm getting old. My police pension kicks in next month, and I'm looking to retire to someplace warm that ain't got any monsters. Maybe Florida."

"Hold up," Kevin balked. "You're really are a cop?"

Abner scowled. "Yes, I'm really a cop. How do you think I found you all from the license plate? Wiggled my nose like 'I Dream of Jeannie?' I keep thinking you kids might not be stupid, and you insist on prove me wrong."

"You kidnapped three people right before your pension kicks in, and you think *we're* stupid?" Woodrow asked.

Abner laughed at that. "Well, wasn't really my intention, but I was kinda impressed by how you handled the thing. And you didn't seem to be complete delinquents, so I had an idea."

Kevin and Woodrow were not excited to hear about any idea Abner had.

"You see, I ain't got any kids. My brother's been gone for twenty years now, and there's no one else left in the family. So if I go, this place don't have no one keeping an eye on it. So you three are here because I feel like it wouldn't be right for me to take off without anyone knowing about it."

"Uh, you want us to take over your job of hunting these things? Are you out of your mind?" Kevin asked.

"Maybe, maybe not. Don't really know if you could even handle it. So that's what we're gonna find out."

"What do you mean by find out?" Woodrow asked.

Abner stood up, gave a little stretch, and looked at his watch. "Well, it's about six-thirty now, so what's gonna happen is I'm gonna head home and then swing back by here tomorrow, and if you're still here, I'm gonna give you the keys to the cabin and a coupla journals that will help you out, and then I'm never gonna come to these woods again. And if you don't make it, well, can't say I didn't try!"

Woodrow laughed this time. "Six-thirty? Man, it can't be more than one in the afternoon."

"You'd think, but light ain't the only thing that works funny in these woods. Check your watch," Abner snickered.

Woodrow glanced at his watch, looked at Kevin for a second, then looked back and stared for a long time. "What the hell?" He held it up so Kevin could see.

It read 6:24 pm.

"Next time you suggest driving up to the Moonies, I'm going home," Kevin said after staring at the watch.

"As you can see, it's time for me to go. I aim to be back home before sunset. You boys don't move for a minute or so, and I'll see myself out.

He tipped his baseball cap and headed out the door.

Chapter Twelve

Shawn watched as the man emerged from the cabin. He shouted, "Let me out of this, you psycho!"

The man smiled at Shawn and said, "You have a nice night now, and if you're lucky, I'll be seeing you tomorrow. Good luck!"

He walked into the woods with his shotgun resting on his shoulder.

A moment later, Kevin and Woodrow burst out of the cabin and looked around.

"Get me the hell out of this!" Shawn yelled.

Woodrow looked over at him and said, "Shawn, we've got a big problem."

"I think we have more than one," Kevin said matter-of-factly as he looked into the woods where Abner had thrown the key.

A howl came from the forest. It didn't sound as far away as they would have liked.

"We've gotta find that key," Woodrow said, "Kevin, go grab those flashlights from the cabin. They'll help.

Kevin ducked back inside, and Woodrow went over and worked the axe out of the stump. He went over to Shawn and handed it to him, "We'll look for the key. In the meantime maybe you can break the chain with this?"

They both looked at the thick chain and then at each other. Shawn said, "Yeah, that's not happening, but maybe I can get it out of the stump."

"Worth a try," Woodrow responded.

There was another howl from a different spot in the woods.

"That was from the other side. I think there's more than one out there," Shawn said with an air of dread in his voice. "What happened in the cabin? Why did he take off like that?"

Kevin came out of the cabin carrying two of the flashlights.

Woodrow said, "We'll fill you in once we find the key or get you loose." He jogged over to Kevin and grabbed one of the flashlights. Together, they headed into the woods where the key had gone.

Shawn began to try and pry the chain free.

The world dimmed almost as soon as Kevin and Woodrow crossed out of the clearing and into the woods. Having been made aware of it, the sense of wrongness felt palpable. Woodrow shuddered.

"It couldn't have gone more than thirty or forty feet," Kevin said, "Assuming it didn't hit anything on its flight."

"We should start about fifty feet in and work our way back. It looked silver, so maybe we'll get lucky, and the light will reflect off it.

Another howl, sounded followed by more from a different direction. They sounded like they were answering each other. Kevin and Woodrow glanced at each other and then frantically searched the forest floor for a glint of metal.

The underbrush was mostly ferns growing through a bed of dead leaves. It wasn't overly thick, but it was enough that it made the task at hand feel daunting to both of them.

They went in as far as they could conceivably imagine the key had gone, then went a little further beyond that. They separated by about five feet and began to methodically walk back toward the cabin. They shone their lights on the ground in arcs and pulled up the ferns as they went.

It was slow going. After about ten feet, Woodrow could feel his heart pounding in his chest. Finding a small key on the forest floor seemed impossible to him, although he didn't want to admit it. He called out to Shawn, "Any luck over there?"

Shawn responded with a frantic yell, "Nope. This thing is in there too deep. I'm going to try and chop it out."

Kevin yelled back, "Just don't break the axe. We're gonna need it."

Woodrow glanced at Kevin questioningly. Kevin responded, "That was the only weapon I saw. He took the shotgun. I'm not sure how effective throwing cans of peas is gonna be."

"Good point," Woodrow responded.

They redoubled their efforts scouring the forest floor. Around them, the daylight dwindled.

Kevin and Woodrow got to the edge of the woods without finding the key. Half an hour had passed, or what they thought was a half an hour. They realized that they had no real way of knowing anymore.

Beyond the edge of the woods, they could hear Shawn grunting and the axe repeatedly striking the stump.

Wordlessly, they spread out a little more and started working their way back into the woods. Although they were trying to ignore it, the howls seemed to be getting more frequent and closer.

"We saw him throw it! Where the hell could it be?" Woodrow said desperately as they got thirty feet into the forest.

"It might have bounced off a tree branch and landed God-only-knows-where," Kevin said. He shined his light up into the trees as he said it. They didn't see a metallic glint, but it did highlight how dark it was getting.

"The sun is setting too fast. This place makes no sense," Woodrow said angrily.

They got back to where they started with no luck. Both of them were getting frantic as they once again turned and walked back toward the cabin, swinging their lights side to side and tearing up any plants along the forest floor they could find.

"This isn't going to work," Woodrow said, "You keep trying. I'm going to check on Shawn and see if he's got any hope of dislodging it."

"You're gonna leave me alone in the woods?" Kevin balked.

"Not for long," Woodrow said and took off at a jog.

Shawn's arms were starting to cramp as he chopped away at the stump.

The chain was embedded so deep into it that it seemed like the stump had grown up around it. He had hit the chain a couple of times with the axe, and that had amounted to nothing more than painful jolts up his arms. It was just too thick.

He rested for a moment and looked up. The sun, which should have been high in the sky based on when they entered the woods, was beginning to set. Shawn did not want to spend a night out in the open chained to a stump.

There was a series of howls from different parts of the forest around him as if to punctuate the thought.

He jumped as he heard Woodrow emerge from the woods noisily. Woodrow came jogging over with a grim look on his face. "No luck with the stump I take it?" he asked.

"I feel like I'm trying to pull the sword from the stone, and I'm not the rightful king. I'm guessing you didn't find the key?" Shawn asked doubtfully.

"Kevin is still looking, but it's getting dark. I think we might be S.O.L. with the key. We're gonna have to figure something else out," Woodrow responded.

"I'm open to any ideas except the ones involving dismemberment or staying out in this forest after the sun sets," Shawn said desperately.

Woodrow shrugged. "I've got nothing yet. I'm going to double-check the cabin for anything we might use."

"Hurry," Shawn said.

Woodrow ran into the cabin and looked around. He looked at the gas heater and wondered briefly if they could set the stump on fire to free it. He thought that would work, but it would take a long time, and they didn't have much left. Nothing else seemed useful.

As he stood there, he heard Kevin yell from the woods. He bolted out of the cabin just in time to see his friend emerge.

"Did you find it?" he asked hopefully.

"Nope," Kevin said wild-eyed, "But I saw something run past. I think we're out of time."

"Shit," Woodrow said. They both turned to Shawn, still whacking away at the stump.

They both stood there at a complete loss until Kevin slapped himself on the forehead and shouted, "Oh, duh!"

"What?" Woodrow nearly shouted.

Kevin ran over to Shawn, shouting, "Shawn, give me the axe and put your head down on top of the stump."

Shawn turned to Kevin and shouted, "Do *what*?"

"We're doing this wrong. Just do it." Kevin said forcefully.

Woodrow was at a complete loss and then all at once understood what Kevin meant to do, "Oh, damn, we're idiots."

"What are you talking about?" Shawn said frantically.

Kevin grabbed the axe from him. "We're gonna break the lock with the axe. We should have done this right away."

Shawn's eyes went wide. "How are you gonna do that?"

"You're gonna lie down and hold as still as humanly possible," Kevin said with an air of confidence.

Shawn started to argue, but a howl too close by for comfort cut him off. He immediately got on his knees and put his head and neck on the stump as best as he could.

"Come hold this still, Wood," Kevin said. Woodrow complied.

They twisted the collar around, so the lock was against the stump. Shawn closed his eyes as Kevin kissed his knuckles and then raised the axe as high as he dared and then brought it down on the padlock.

There was a metal-on-metal sound, and the lock nearly broke.

Kevin brought the axe up again and then down as hard as he could.

The padlock snapped in half.

Woodrow worked it free of the neck clamp, and they pulled it open. Shawn took a deep breath and stood up. He grabbed Kevin, who was still holding the axe, and hugged him.

"Thank God. Now let's get out…" Woodrow stopped mid-sentence.

They all turned to the edge of the woods thirty feet beyond them as a monster the likes of which they had never imagined stepped into the clearing.

It looked at them with glowing eyes and howled.

CHAPTER THIRTEEN

The Glawackus was the size of an adult bear, with a torso almost as thick. Its legs and arms were long and muscular, with an almost-but-not-quite-human shape to them. Its feet were somewhere between a cat and a wolf but with long, hooked claws extending from the toes. Its arms ended in appendages that looked more like hands than paws. It wasn't apparent if it had thumbs, but what was obvious were the three-inch long claws that extended out from each of the five fingers.

Its head was monstrous. It had a thick mane like a lion, the same as the smaller one that they hit, and the same flat snout, which seemed to resemble a dog, a cat, and a bear all at once.

The eyes were the most horrifying. They glowed a sickly and demented amber, and behind the glow, they were black as night with an intelligence in them that frightened Woodrow to his core.

There was a moment frozen in time as they stared at each other before they all three broke at once for the cabin. The Glawackus, which had walked into the clearing on its hind legs like a man, dropped onto all fours and loped after them.

Shawn got to the door first, threw it open, and dove in. Woodrow followed him and grabbed the door. As soon as Kevin was through, Woodrow slammed it shut and put his back against it. There was a crash, and he could feel the wood nearly buckle, but it held.

Kevin added his weight against the door, bracing for another blow. It was a few seconds coming, but when it did, the door strained even more.

Shawn ran over and swept everything off the table. He pushed it over to brace against the door. It was a sturdy, hand-built hardwood table but he had no trouble moving with the amount of adrenaline coursing through his system.

A third crash came, but this one was less powerful than the first two. The door held.

"Move and help me flip this up against the door," Shawn yelled.

Kevin stayed pressed against the door, but Woodrow moved to help Shawn. They turned the table on its end and braced it. Kevin got out of the way at the last second.

"I think that was one of the big ones he mentioned," Woodrow said.

"I really hope so," Kevin replied, "If they get any bigger, we're in deep trouble."

There was another howl from just outside the house.

"I think we're in deep trouble already," Shawn said softly.

The Glawackus tried to push the door open two more times before it stopped. The table held, but none of them thought the door itself could withstand many more blows.

The cabin two windows were probably too small for the cryptid to fit through, but Kevin and Woodrow had stationed themselves by them just in case. Shawn remained by the door, leaning against the table and holding the axe with a white-knuckled grip.

There wasn't much else they were able to use as weapons in the cabin. Woodrow wielded one of the flashlights and wished it was one of the big, heavy ones that cops carried instead of a flimsier, shorter version. Shawn had pulled apart the metal cot and was holding one of the hollow metal bars from it like a bat.

They could see the thing prowling around the cabin from the windows. It switched between walking on two legs and all fours seemingly at random. It occasionally looked at the cabin and howled a piercing howl that set their teeth on edge every time.

The sun had gone fully down, and the moon had risen, casting the whole clearing in a baleful glow. It was easy to keep track of the cryptid even in the lower light because its eyes seemed to glow brighter as the night progressed.

Kevin, Shawn, and Woodrow had all remained largely silent as time stretched out. The tension of waiting for an attack to come kept them on edge but was also rapidly exhausting them.

"I don't get it. Why doesn't it attack?" Shawn finally asked, breaking the silence.

"Beats me, but I'm not about to complain," Kevin responded.

"When it…" Woodrow began. "When it came into the clearing, its eyes looked, not human, but smart. Like it was assessing the situation and, I dunno, recognized us?"

"Yeah," Shawn agreed, "Not like it knew who we were, but like, it knew we were human and what we were all about."

"It looked at us like dinner," Kevin said, "Like its favorite dinner at that."

"It's so different from the one we hit," Shawn said, his voice shaky. "That one looked like a dog. This looks like a werewolf or something."

"Yeah, except not just a wolf," Woodrow answered, "Like a bear, wolf, cat, and dog all mashed up, but also sorta human."

"It looked like it had thumbs under all those claws," Kevin observed.

They all shuddered involuntarily at the thought of the claws. Shawn whispered, "So many claws."

Another howl from outside.

They went quiet for a few minutes.

"So what do we do?" Shawn asked.

Kevin and Woodrow both shrugged before Woodrow answered, "I think our best bet is to try and get through the night, and then if it leaves in the morning, we make a break for it."

"Make a break for it?" Kevin asked.

"Yeah, what's-his-face, Abner left not long before it got dark, and he seemed to imply they were mostly nocturnal," Woodrow answered.

"That guy's name was *Abner*?" Shawn said with some surprise.

Kevin and Woodrow exchanged a glance, both realizing that Shawn hadn't heard most of the story Abner had told.

"Yeah, I guess we oughta tell you what he told us while you were chained up." Kevin ventured.

"What kinda stupid name is Abner?" Shawn snarked.

Woodrow gave a small, weak laugh. "About as stupid as Woodrow."

"So that's about it. He wants us to take over his job of, I guess, caretaking this place and hunting down strays," Kevin finished.

Shawn looked from Kevin to Woodrow and then back, dumbfounded. "I'm not alone in thinking that's utterly insane, right?"

Woodrow shook his head. "I don't think Abner is quite right in the head, which, given that he spends a lot of time in the woods alone with cryptids, kinda makes sense."

"You think he's telling the truth?" Kevin asked.

"I don't know, but my guess is probably?" Woodrow continued, "We've seen the cryptids, we saw the weird time shit, and we all feel how… bad… this place feels."

There was another howl outside, followed by two more in quick succession that were very close by. All three of them tightened their grips on their improvised weapons. Shawn looked out the window and yelped.

"What?" Kevin asked, leaning harder against the bracing table.

"There's two more out there." he replied, his tone flat. "They are pacing, like, cats I guess. They're on all fours."

Woodrow glanced out his window. "The other one is still there. It's pacing too…" A howl cut him off.

Shawn shuddered at the sound. "That howling is making me feel insane. I wish they would stop."

"At least when they're howling, they're not attacking," Kevin offered, struggling to keep the fear out of his voice. "If they all attack the cabin…" he didn't need to finish.

No one spoke for a while. The night was quiet other than the periodic howling. The Glawackuses—Glawacki?—were not silent in their movement either, so the boys found they could hear the sound of them padding around the cabin. After some time had passed Woodrow took another glance out.

"There's more now," he said, "looks like three or four of the smaller ones."

Shawn hazarded a glance. "Christ, there's a few over here. They're just sitting there."

"The big ones, too?" Kevin asked.

Woodrow answered, "They're still pacing." He squinted and realized there were even more sitting along the edge of the woods. "Oh my god. There's like ten of them out there. Look by the woods."

"I don't want to look anymore," Shawn said. "There's nothing we can do against that many. I feel like a mouse in a house full of cats."

No one said anything, the realization of their danger fully hitting them.

After a few moments, Kevin started, "Hey guys," he paused for several seconds as if trying to figure out the right words. "If we don't make it. I just. I want to say, I..." He stopped again. "You're my best friends, I don't know what I'd do without you, and I'm kinda terrified of you leaving for school, or was I guess. Now I'm just terrified period."

Woodrow tried to come up with a response. Finally, he said, "Yeah, me too. It's scary, like I'm going to Boston, and yeah, I know a couple of people there, but it isn't the same."

"Like, half the class is going to UConn," Shawn added. "So I'm not gonna be alone, but also, yeah, it won't be the same."

"I just feel like I'm being left behind, and it sucks. I know you're not that far, but..." Kevin said.

"Yeah," Woodrow said, "we get it."

They let silence fall again, not really knowing what else to say.

CHAPTER FOURTEEN

"Why do you think they haven't attacked?" Shawn asked, breaking the prolonged silence.

Kevin offered, "Maybe they're waiting for their king."

Shawn and Woodrow both stared at him.

"I mean, it's possible," Kevin said with a shrug.

"Yeah, but I really don't want to think about an even *bigger* one," Shawn said.

"I wonder if it has anything to do with the shit on the ceiling?" Woodrow said and then turned the flashlight on and pointed it up. They all followed the beam. "I thought they were just scratches before, but after sitting here staring at it for a while, it's a pattern."

Kevin stared up. "Still looks like scratch marks to me."

"Yeah, but they repeat," Woodrow said and traced the light along the edges of the pattern he was seeing. "It kinda looks like letters or symbols, but I dunno what kind."

Shawn watched as the light traveled across the ceiling. "Yeah, I see it. They're basically in circles, but without the edges drawn," he paused thoughtfully, "You think it's a ward or something?"

"A ward?" Kevin asked.

Shawn nodded in the darkness. "Yeah, like a symbol that keeps stuff out. Kinda like a dreamcatcher. Don't you have one of those hanging in your living room?"

"Pretty sure my mom bought that because it was pretty, not to keep demon bear-cat-dogs at bay," Kevin said doubtfully.

Woodrow answered, "Well yeah, sure, but technically, they're supposed to keep bad dreams away. Maybe these are wards to keep demon bear-cat-dogs out."

"God knows I don't believe in magic and shit, but like, he obviously slept here right?" Kevin said, "There's a cot, a space heater, and food." He eyed the bar in his hand. "Well, *was* a cot anyway."

"Huh. I hadn't thought of that," Kevin said before he stood up fully and stopped leaning against the table and door. He started to walk over to where Shawn was.

"What are you doing?" Woodrow asked hastily.

"I just want to see outside," Kevin said and looked out the window.

Outside, the clearing was filled with fifteen, possibly twenty Glawackuses. They were sitting in cat-like fashion, all staring in at the cabin with glowing eyes. None of them were moving any longer.

"Whaaaaaaat the hell?" Kevin said.

"Maybe they're hoping we come out." Woodrow offered. He glanced at his watch, "Guys, my watch says it's almost 5:30."

"That's it?" Shawn said, "Feels like we've been in here fifteen hours."

Woodrow shrugged, "Maybe we have. It doesn't make sense. But I think the sun starts to come up about now, right?" He switched off his flashlight and looked out the window, trying to determine if it was any lighter out.

"Think they'll go away when the sun comes up?" Kevin asked.

"I couldn't begin to guess," Woodrow answered.

They fell silent and waited for dawn.

Woodrow's watch hit 5:30 am, and he squinted at the sky through the window, hoping to see some sign of light.

With agonizing slowness, the darkness outside began to break. They could almost make out the tops of the trees as the morning light began to grow.

Fifteen minutes passed as the world grew brighter around them. The three of them gathered at the window they thought was facing east and felt their hopes crash as the cryptids outside didn't move. They sat in their same spots, staring at the cabin.

"What if they don't g..." Shawn began to say just as the largest of the Glawackus began to howl. Seconds passed before another joined in, then another, and another. Soon, they all joined in a deafening, eardrum-piercing chorus. The boys stepped back from the windows and covered their ears against the noise. As they began to brace themselves for an attack, the one that began the howl stopped, stood up, and walked into the trees.

One after the other, the remaining Glawackus stood up on their hind legs, or all fours for the smaller ones, and disappeared into the woods. Finally, only one remained. Rather than retreat into the woods, it walked closer to the window where the three of them stood. It was one of the adult ones, walking on its hind legs. It stared in at them with its glowing, amber eyes.

They met its gaze.

Woodrow shook his head and blinked at the sudden bright light. He was standing at the window with Kevin and Shawn next to him. They were both looking out the window and standing still.

"What the hell?" he said, and at the sound of his voice, Kevin and Shawn both stirred and shook their heads as if waking up.

Looking out the window it was fully light, and there was no sign of the Glawackus. Woodrow glanced at his watch, and it was nine-thirty in the morning.

"Uhhhhh, what happened?" Kevin asked.

"I have no earthly idea," Woodrow responded.

"We were looking out the window at the one that walked over, and that's all I remember," Shawn said.

"Same," Kevin replied.

Woodrow nodded, "Yeah, me too."

"Well, that's pretty weird!" Shawn said loudly, his voice shaky and agitated.

Woodrow looked out one window, then over to the other. "They all seem to be gone," he said.

"I tell you what, guys," Kevin said, scratching his chest and tightening his grip on the axe, "I've had about enough of this place, and I want to go home."

"Yeah," Shawn agreed. "They're gone. I say we make a break for it and follow that trail out of here."

Woodrow tossed the flashlight he was holding onto the floor. "Works for me." He turned toward the door and noticed for the first time that the table was moved to the side and the door was slightly ajar. "What... the... hell?"

They all three paused for a moment, staring at the door that had been barred shut with the table.

"You know what?" Shawn asked rhetorically. "I don't care." He lifted the bar from the cot into a position to hit anything that jumped at him and pulled the door open.

Nothing happened.

He turned and looked back. "Let's go."

With that, he walked outside. The other two followed, braced for an attack that did not come.

Chapter Fifteen

They found the trail without much trouble. Exhausted from the last twenty-four hours, even with some level of adrenaline, they had to take it slow.

The trail had been hard to follow on the way in, and that proved doubly true on the way out. Several times, they had to stop and rest, as well as double back after taking a wrong turn.

After half an hour of walking roughly a mile in Woodrow's estimation, they had to stop and rest.

"Does any of this seem familiar?" he asked, sitting on the trunk of a dead tree.

Shawn shrugged. "It all looks the same to me, but maybe a little?"

"This is definitely the right way," Kevin responded. "I remember the log you're sitting on. There aren't that many dead trees around here."

Woodrow looked around. "Yeah, I guess you're right. I think my head is still a little fuzzy from whatever happened back there."

Kevin agreed. "Yeah, same. I feel like I woke up from a nap. Sorta disoriented."

"I feel like I was watching a movie, and the reel skipped a scene or two," Shawn said. "Maybe they're aliens, and they kidnapped us and probed us."

"My ass doesn't feel like it's been probed," Kevin said, "Feels like I've been clenching it for twenty-four straight hours."

They all chuckled a little. It was a nervous laugh but genuine.

"What time is it?" Shawn asked.

"10:15," Woodrow answered, "I keep looking at it, and it hasn't jumped at all again."

"Huh," Shawn replied. "Maybe time is only funny when you're going in one direction?"

"Well, we oughta keep going in the opposite direction then." Kevin said, "We've already been gone a whole day without calling. I dunno about you guys, but my mom is going to *flip*."

"Christ," Shawn said, "I hadn't thought of that."

"We gotta get home before anyone can flip out," Woodrow said while standing up, "I guess we oughta get moving again."

They took a few more short rests and felt the weight of the night begin to lift off their shoulders as the miles went by.

"The forest feels different here," Kevin said. "Less, I dunno how to describe it, heavy?"

"It just seems like a normal place," Shawn offered as they walked.

"There's birds too," Woodrow said, "There weren't birds in the bad part."

They walked a while longer without losing the path. It was small but much harder to lose at this point.

They heard a car drive by in the near distance.

"Oh, thank God," Shawn said and began to walk faster.

Eventually, they saw the Thunderbird through the woods and broke out into the daylight.

Abner's Jeep was nowhere to be seen.

Shawn was so happy he went up and kissed his car.

The relief hit them like a physical blow. Feeling the tension leave their bodies Kevin and Woodrow sat down on the ground.

Woodrow felt like crying until he heard Shawn say, "What the hell is this?"

Shawn had opened the front door of the car and was now holding up several old-looking books.

Kevin and Woodrow looked at each other, remembering Abner had mentioned leaving them some journals.

There was a note sticking out of one of them. Shawn pulled it out and read it: "Hope you boys had a lovely night. I changed my mind about waiting for you. Good luck." He crumbled it up and tossed it into the woods. "I don't like that guy much."

"I think littering is a $50 fine," Woodrow pointed out.

"Shut up." Shawn snapped with a laugh.

Chapter Sixteen

They sat in the car in front of the Glastonbury police station, debating how to proceed.

After significant discussion they had concluded that they needed to find Abner before they went back home. He had told them he was a cop and the badge he had flashed Shawn in Stamford had said Glastonbury.

Kevin and Shawn were in front, while Woodrow was in the back looking through the books. They turned out to be a history of Glastonbury and two journals that appeared to have belonged to Abner's grandfather and father, assuming he had not lied to them about who he was.

"Ready to go in?" Kevin asked.

"As I'll ever be, I guess," Shawn said, "How about you, Wood? Anything interesting in the books?"

Woodrow snapped the journal he was looking at shut. "Yeah, I think? It would all sound insane if we hadn't seen what we've seen."

"You sure we're not insane?" Kevin asked as he opened the door and climbed from the car. He flipped his seat forward to let Woodrow out, "Hopefully, there isn't a statewide APB out for us."

Shawn laughed. "Probably not, but at least we look like shit."

Woodrow looked down at his clothes. They were scratched and torn in a few spots and covered in dirt and detritus. "Glastonbury rich enough that they lock up vagrants?"

"Beats me," Kevin responded, "Will probably just give us the bums rush."

They closed the doors and walked into the station. The brick building looked brand new with inviting gleaming white doors. The three of them, who were used to getting yelled at by Stamford's police, couldn't help but feel weird walking into a police station on purpose.

At the information desk sat a young woman officer who didn't look much older than them. Her nameplate read "Officer Hanson." There was no one else in the main reception room or on the benches by the door.

She eyed them up as they walked up. "Can I help you, fellas?" she said in a pleasant but wary voice.

They looked at each other, not having rehearsed what to say, before Woodrow spoke up, "Good morning, officer," he looked at the nameplate again, having already forgotten what it said, "Hanson." He paused and cleared his throat. Talking to the police always made him feel incredibly guilty. "We're here to see Detective Johnson?"

"That sounds a bit like the start of a dirty joke," Officer Hanson remarked.

Woodrow started to explain it wasn't a prank when she cut him off, "I know, I know, just busting your chops. You young men seem a little nervous."

None of them responded. She sighed, "Well, thing is, we have a couple of Detective Johnsons here."

"Uh," Kevin started before she laughed.

"That definitely sounded like a joke," she said, "But seriously, we've got two. Or did, I guess."

Woodrow raised his eyebrow when she said 'did' and then said, "Uh, Abner Johnson."

"Figures," she responded, "You missed Detective Abner Johnson by about a week. He retired and, as far as I know, began his long trek to Florida."

"Seriously?" Shawn blurted.

"'Fraid so!" Officer Hanson replied, "We had a party and everything."

"Well, shit," Kevin said.

"Can I interest you in a different detective? Were you looking to report a crime?"

Kevin, Shawn, and Woodrow looked at each other, sharing an unspoken communication, before Woodrow said, "No, thank you. We just had to talk to him about some town history and camping in the forest. He had offered to, uh," he thought for a second, "to give us some advice."

The officer gave them an incredulous look before saying, "Are you sure you're talking about *Abner* Johnson?" She emphasized his name.

"Definitely sure," Woodrow responded.

"Are you family friends of his?" she asked.

"Just acquaintances," Woodrow said.

"Well, I guess you live and learn," Officer Hanson replied, "Between you and me and the wall, I always thought he was kind of a prick. Didn't seem like the friendly advice type."

"Well, that tracks," Shawn snarked before asking, "Did he leave a forwarding address or anything?"

"Sure did. I can grab that for you," she said before getting up and walking through a door into the back area.

They waited a few minutes before she came back with an address written on a business card. "Here you go. Hopefully, he's a nicer pen pal than a co-worker." She handed Woodrow the card, "I'm gonna go ahead and offer you boys some advice."

She grinned as they all looked nervous. "Next time you wander into a police station to talk to a cop, maybe get cleaned up first. You look like you slept in the woods."

Shawn put on Metallica's Black album and skipped ahead to "Of Wolf and Man." Turning the volume up, he drove away from Glastonbury as fast as he could.

When they hit the highway south, "Enter Sandman" came on, and they all shouted along to the lyrics, releasing what remained of their tension into the warm June air flowing through the rolled-down windows.

They kept the music cranked and the windows down and shouted and sang along to most of the album as they went. It had been a favorite of theirs since it had come out and had never been so cathartic.

After a second round of "Of Wolf and Man," which felt like it held new meaning for all of them, Shawn turned down the radio and said, "Let's stop and get something to eat before we go home. I could eat a horse."

"We're almost to Norwalk," Woodrow said, "Let's stop at the Silver Star."

"I could do something unpleasant to a plate of hash and eggs right about now," Kevin said. "Plus, we can call our folks from there."

"Good idea," Woodrow said, "I'm just gonna tell Mom I stayed at your place, Kevin, and that I forgot to call."

"Works for me. I'll tell my folks I stayed at your place."

Shawn nodded. "I'll tell mine I stayed at yours, Kevin. Or I guess we could tell them the truth."

"Uhhh, I don't know about that," Woodrow said.

Kevin laughed. "There's no chance of telling them the truth. First off, they won't believe me. Second, it makes us sound insane, or like we're trying to cover up some truly heinous shit."

"Yeah, I guess. It feels weird not to tell anyone that we got kidnapped by a cop, though, ya know?" Shawn said, "Is there anyone we can or should tell, or are we just stuck with this?"

Neither Kevin nor Woodrow had a good answer to that question.

They rode in silence until they got to the diner, just off the highway on the Post Road. As they got out, Woodrow grabbed the journals from the back and brought them.

"Here you go, two plates of hash and eggs, one sunny side up, one over easy," the waitress said as she laid down an impressive number of plates. "And here you go, darling, one chicken parm."

Woodrow could hear his stomach growl as he looked lustily at the food in front of him. Kevin and Shawn took turns calling and getting yelled at by their parents. It wasn't unusual for them to be out until two or three in the morning, but it was abnormal for them not to be there in the morning without a call.

While everyone else was on the phone Woodrow looked through the journal of Abner's grandfather.

"So what does it say?" Kevin said through a mouthful of toast.

Woodrow swallowed an enormous bite before saying, "It starts out with what I assume is Abner's grandfather getting handed the job of 'guarding the woods' by his older brother, who died shortly after, it sounds like."

"He give him the job by locking him in a cabin in the woods at night, too?" Kevin said sarcastically.

"Nah, he just tells him what to do, I think. It's kinda hard to read the handwriting, and the spelling is pretty creative. I don't think Abner's grandfather did a lot of reading and writing after going to grade school. He does mention a house in the woods, though."

"That cabin didn't look all that old," Shawn said.

Woodrow shrugged. "Maybe they rebuilt it or something. I only read a couple of pages. But check this out." He held up the journal and showed them a drawing on the page.

It was the symbol that they had seen on the roof of the cabin.

"Well shit, so it really is something," Kevin said, "What does it say about it?"

Woodrow read for a second, "Just says it's 'The Glyph,' doesn't say for what."

"The heck is a glyph?" asked Kevin.

"Like a rune. A magic design, I guess," Woodrow replied and read further. "It makes a point that the Wangunk…"

"The what?" Shawn interrupted.

"The Wangunk, the local indigenous tribe," Woodrow said, "Sorry, I keep forgetting you were, uh, outside for most of his story." He continued, "Anyway, it says it's not a Wangunk thing. They just gave it to his family. They apparently got it from someone else."

"Who?" Shawn asked.

Woodrow scanned the rest of the page and the next. He flipped quickly, scanning a couple more pages. "Doesn't say."

"That's weird. Who else would have been there?"

That question hung in the air until Woodrow snapped the book shut and turned back to his meal. "You know what, that's enough of that. I'm so tired my eyes are getting blurry reading it."

They finished up their food, settled up at the counter, and headed out for the last stretch home.

Shawn dropped Kevin off first and then Woodrow. All three got home and immediately crawled into bed. Their parents wouldn't be home from work until later in the day, so they had time to sleep.

Chapter Seventeen

Woodrow spent the next couple of days reading the journals and the book. Things had returned to a state of semi-normalcy. Their parents' annoyance at their brief disappearance dissipated quickly. Woodrow's Mom had gone to see Jurassic Park on her own, though.

The guys all had to work that week but they still checked in every night and planned to get together again on Friday, as usual.

The book, a locally written history of Glastonbury, had not proven to be particularly interesting or useful in better understanding what had happened. By the end of it, Woodrow was convinced that Abner had left it simply because it mentioned his family in positive ways and, toward the end, had made a note of his being an Eagle Scout and a police detective. The only thing Woodrow had found interesting in reading it was how many missing persons it mentioned in passing, including one of the town's mayors in the early part of the century.

The journals held more information but didn't truly hold many answers. There were three passages the grandfather, Mordecai Johnson, had written that Woodrow had bookmarked to read to Kevin and Shawn.

The first was just a basic description of the cryptid, but it gave it a different name than Glawackus, which made sense since that name wasn't coined until the '30s. The original name was "Nénepómsha Renna," which was apparently what the Wangunk had called it. The journal didn't say what that meant. Woodrow assumed it didn't involve the word 'wacky.'

The second was about the symbol. Early in the journal Grandpa Johnson wrote that the Wangunk had given it to him, but a later passage mentioned that he found it on rocks in a cave and once on a tree.

Specifically, he wrote that it had been hacked into a tree, whatever that meant. It made the symbol seem important.

This reinforced Woodrow's belief that the reason the Glawackuses never came into the cabin was the symbol on the ceiling. He did wonder why it was carved inside the building and not on the outside. He didn't know anything about symbology, but he did know that in the Bible, people had marked their doors on the outside to get the Angel of Death to leave them alone.

The third entry he had noted was about the Glawackus hysteria in the '30s. Mordecai wrote that one of the younger ones had left the forest, similar to the one they hit in Pound Ridge, and went on a little tear, getting itself seen in the process. It amused Woodrow that of all the hoaxes and hysterias about monsters around the world, the one from Connecticut turned out to be true.

It also mentioned that Mordecai had broken its leg when he captured it and brought back. Abner had mentioned that he used tranquilizers because the creatures were hard to kill, and this just seemed to confirm that.

Abner's father's journal was much less interesting. Very little of it was actually about the Glawackus or the woods. It was mostly about raising Abner and his brother Ezekial. The entries made him seem like a decent father to Woodrow, and he wondered if he was disappointed that Abner grew up into a prick.

What stood out was one of the last entries. The previous entry had mentioned that their father thought Ezekial was ready, although he didn't write for what exactly, but it was implied there was something that sounded like a ceremony. The next entry simply said that Ezekial had failed, and that Abner would have to be the one. After that, there was a long gap in the dates of the entries. The rest were mostly about Abner being an Eagle Scout until the last entry, which just said, "Abner is ready."

When Abner had been talking to them in the cabin, he had made a comment about his brother disappearing. Woodrow hadn't thought about it much, but now he wondered why Abner had glossed over that part and what the stuff about being ready was all about.

After reading all three books, Woodrow had more questions than answers and it didn't seem like there was much chance of changing that anytime soon.

None of them had to work that Friday, so they got together early in the afternoon to play basketball. Jodie's birthday party was that night, and they had decided they were all going to go, so they wanted to talk ahead of time.

As they played, Woodrow shared what he had read in the journals and the book. Kevin was interested in the symbol and a bit disappointed that the volumes didn't contain much information on them.

"It hadn't occurred to me that the monster would have a different name, but I guess that makes a lot of sense," Shawn said as he shot a free throw. "What did you say it was again?" There were only three of them there, so they were playing 21.

"Don't make me try and pronounce it again," Woodrow laughed.

Kevin grabbed the rebound and dribbled back out to reset. "Sounds sexier than Glawackus at least." He took a quick dribble and jab step at Woodrow and then launched a shot. It swished through the net, "That's 21, gentlemen," he said before tapping his fist on his chest and wincing a little. "Or I guess 63 in this case."

Shawn and Woodrow both groaned. It was the third straight game Kevin had won. They all enjoyed playing, but Kevin was quite a bit better than they were.

They took a break, grabbed some Gatorade, and sat on the grass next to the court. They were silent for a minute until Kevin said, "You guys been sleeping okay since, uh, all of that?"

Woodrow shrugged. "Yeah, about the same as normal."

Shawn nodded. "Ditto. Guessing you're not?"

"Yeah, I've been having dreams about it ever since. Vivid ones." Kevin said.

"Nightmares?" Shawn asked.

Kevin made a face, "Ennnh, not really. Weirder. I don't wake up in a cold sweat screaming or anything, but they're intense."

"I mean, we got held at gunpoint and saw a bunch of cryptids. Seems like that might have some effect." Woodrow offered. "I haven't had dreams, but I've been a bit jumpy."

"I'm not looking forward to driving up to North Stamford tonight for this party if we're being honest," Shawn said, "Gonna be a while before I wanna drive in the woods again, I think."

"Speaking of," Kevin interjected, changing the subject. "I made an appointment for my license. My dad is gonna buy a new car finally, so I'll inherit the Pontiac."

"Isn't that kind of a piece of shit?" Shawn asked.

"Sure, but it'll get me around, and it'll be my piece of shit. And no more buses." Kevin said happily.

"Gonna actually study for that test, or you need me to do the reading for you again?" Woodrow asked.

Shawn snorted, and Kevin laughed and threw the basketball from his lap at Woodrow. He dodged, but it knocked the Gatorade bottle from his hand, which dumped the contents all over Shawn.

They all doubled over laughing.

As the summer went on, things got back to normal. The events of that night faded, and they talked about it less and less. College became the main topic of conversation when they got together. Shawn and Woodrow spent more and more time focusing on the fall and getting ready. By the beginning of August, they hardly mentioned the encounter in the woods at all.

The days drifted by, and melancholy and desperation began to set in. All of their laughter and silliness held an edge. They all felt it, although none of them really knew how to articulate it. And ending seemed to be rushing up to meet them and that was somehow scarier than that night in the woods.

Finally, the summer drew to a close. Woodrow and Shawn were both set to head off to school on the same day, a Thursday in late August. The night before, they all met at their favorite diner out on High Ridge Road. They didn't say a lot, just enjoying what time they had left.

After settling up, they left the diner and headed down to the beach at Cove Island to share a bottle of Yukon Jack that Shawn's brother had left behind.

"I'm gonna miss you guys," Woodrow said into the ocean breeze. "I don't know what I'm going to do without you."

"Yeah," Shawn replied, "Same."

"You're going to Boston and Storrs, guys," Kevin said, "Not Vietnam."

They all laughed and were quiet again for a while.

"Seriously though," Kevin began, "We're not that far away. You'll visit home, and I'll come up and hang out with you on campus. And you're gonna make new friends."

"Sure," said Woodrow, "But it won't be the same."

"Nah," Kevin agreed. "It'll never be the same, but that's kind of the point, right? If it stayed the same it would go stale and eventually rotten. We're always gonna look back on this time fondly, but the only way to look back is to move forward."

Shawn and Woodrow both turned and looked at Kevin. "Who the hell are you, and what have you done with Kevin?" Woodrow asked with a laugh.

"I had a lot of time to think about this when I *wasn't* packing for college," Kevin chuckled. "But seriously, I was dreading you guys going away, and still am, but I think it'll be good, and I'll figure out my own way too."

Shawn raised the bottle and said, "Alright, guys, to the future," and took a sip. He passed the bottle to Kevin, who echoed Shawn's words, "To the future," before handing it to Woodrow. Woodrow took the bottle and said, "The future. L'chaim!" before downing the last swig. He reached back and threw the bottle as hard as he could toward the water.

Together, they watched the waves crash onto the sand.

Kevin slept in on the morning Shawn and Woodrow left. The dreams that had plagued him earlier in the summer had mostly gone away, but that night, he had tossed and turned. He had woken up two or three times, half expecting to see one of the Glawackus in his room.

Around eleven o'clock, he finally crawled out of bed. After some breakfast and a shower, he tossed on some jeans, a Pearl Jam t-shirt he bought when he saw them in New York in December, and a flannel that was probably too heavy for the late August weather.

Once dressed, he grabbed the backpack he had packed up the day before from his closet. He methodically went through it, once again checking its contents. The Maglite worked. There were plenty of granola bars, and the hunting knife he had bought the previous week was still carefully tucked in its sheath. Everything seemed ready to go.

The three books Abner left them were on his nightstand. He tossed them into the pack, too.

He glanced out his window to make sure his parents' cars were both gone. After confirming no one was home, he locked up the house, got in his car, and headed north. "A Man Without" by the Mighty Mighty Bosstones was cranked at top volume as he hit the highway.

He thought again about that morning in the woods as he drove up.

They were crowded around the window as the remaining Glawackus walked up and stared at them with glowing amber eyes. As he looked into those eyes, Kevin saw an intelligence. He stepped back from the window, terrified.

Shawn and Woodrow didn't move. At all.

"What the *hell*?" Kevin exclaimed.

There was no response. He looked away from the window and at his friends. They stood looking out the window, transfixed. They were breathing but otherwise stood frozen. Kevin could see their knuckles white from gripping the flashlight and pole from the cot, but they held perfectly still.

Kevin looked back out the window but saw that the monster was gone. He grabbed Woodrow and shook him by the shoulder. His friend swayed but didn't react.

"Come on, guys, what's going on?" he said frantically.

There was a bang. Kevin turned in time to see the table that had been bracing the door fly to the side, and the door slam open. Outside stood the Glawackus.

Kevin swore and then moved between the monster and his friends. He brandished the axe as menacing as he could muster, expecting the monster to lunge.

It watched him with those strange, glowing eyes for a moment before stepping slowly into the cabin. It stood just inside the door, no more than six feet from Kevin.

He could smell it's sour, hot breath. It didn't have the same awful stench as the smaller one. It smelled like the earth rot of the deep woods.

"Get out!" Kevin shouted at it, swinging the axe in its direction.

It just stared at him, breathing heavily.

The seconds stretched out to what felt like hours to Kevin before it suddenly moved faster than he could have imagined.

The creature darted forward at the same time, rearing its long, muscled arm back. Kevin raised the axe to block the blow, and the force sent the weapon flying across the room. He turned briefly to watch the axe sail out of his hands and then felt the hand close around his throat. His eyes bulged in terror as the thing lifted him by his neck and pushed him against the wall of the cabin.

It held him fast but not so tight that he couldn't breathe. It drew its face close to his and sniffed him several times. He looked away from the monster to Shawn and Woodrow, hoping beyond hope that they had woken up. They still stood there, unmoving.

The monster raised its free hand and reached toward Kevin's chest. Mola Rom from Indiana Jones and the Temple of Doom popped into his head as he felt the monster's claw reach under his t-shirt and press against his chest. He closed his eyes and gritted his teeth, expecting these to be his last moments.

The monster began to drag its claw across his chest in a circular fashion. It hurt, but slowly, he realized it wasn't pushing its talons into his chest. It was carving something into his skin. For agonizing seconds, he felt those knife-like claws as they moved across his chest. Finally, it withdrew its hand and then let go of his neck.

He slumped to the floor.

The Glawackus watched him for a moment and then turned and strode out of the cabin.

Kevin's mind slowly caught up to the fact that he wasn't dead, and he leapt up and ran over to get the axe and then went to the door.

He watched as the Glawackus walked away into the woods. He dropped the axe and pulled off his shirt.

On his chest, carved into him by the claws of a monster, was the same symbol that had been carved over and over into the ceiling of the cabin.

He grabbed one of the water bottles that had been on the table, opened it, and poured the contents over his chest to clean the wound as best he could, and then stared at it.

He felt faint. Overwhelmed by the bizarre encounter.

He sat down on the floor and leaned against the wall of the cabin for a long time. Shawn and Woodrow never moved.

After a while, he saw them start to breathe heavier, and their grip on their improvised weapons loosened. They were waking up from whatever spell the Glawackus had put them under.

For reasons he didn't fully understand, he knew he had to keep what had happened a secret. He used another water bottle to clean the blood off his chest and then put his shirt back on. Before he went to stand where he had been, he grabbed the axe.

When they woke up, he pretended to wake up, too.

It had taken all summer, several read-throughs of the journals, and an endless series of dreams before Kevin understood what had happened.

The journals had talked obliquely about a ceremony and Abner being chosen. Kevin believed that to be what had happened. Abner had taken them into the woods the same way he had been taken, and his brother before him.

Why Kevin had been chosen, and not Shawn or Woodrow, was a mystery to him. Why the monster had left them alone when it apparently took Abner's brother made even less sense, and like most of the other questions, he didn't expect to find answers.

What he did know was that since that day, he could feel the woods pulling at him. He felt drawn there. He tried to ignore it. Convinced himself he was imagining things, but it did no good.

He waited until Woodrow and Shawn had gone before returning. They would have tried to talk him out of it, or would have insisted on coming along. They had new paths to travel on with college, and now he had found his.

He exited the highway and drove through Glastonbury back to the place where they had parked months ago with a monster in their trunk.

He parked as deep in the pull-off as he could and sat in the car for a while, listening to the radio and looking into the woods. "Tom Sawyer" by Rush came on the classic rock radio station he had tuned to. He listened to the song and thought about the story the lyrics told about a man striding through the world as an individual and with purpose. After the final notes, he turned the car off and got out.

He grabbed his backpack, tossed it over his shoulder, and strode into the woods to find his destiny.

About the Author

Jacob Jones-Goldstein, founding member of Oddity Prodigy Productions, is an internationally published author, journalist, and editor. His short stories have appeared in anthologies and magazines such as *Plague of Shadows* from Smart Rhino Press, *Beach Pulp* from Cat & Mouse Press, and *Lovecraftiana* from Rogue Planet Press. His debut novel, *The Change*, will be released in July 2025.

He has edited the volumes *Scary Stuff, Beneath the Yellow Lights,* and *Bright Mirror* for Oddity Prodigy Productions, and is hard at work on their upcoming anthology 'Where Legends Walk.'

In addition to fiction, Jacob writes about music for his personal site, ShoutingStreet.com, and has covered the Philadelphia 76ers for several online publications. Beyond writing and editing, he hosts the popular "The Scary Stuff Podcast," plays Magic the Gathering, Disc Golf, and way too many board games.

He loves comic books, movies, exploring, cats, family, friends, Joel Embiid, Tyrese Maxey, and his wife, Jennie.

artist's rendition of a Glawackus

THE GLAWACKUS

(ALSO KNOWN AS THE NORTHERN DEVIL CAT, GRANBY PANTHER, INJUN DEVIL, GLASTONBURY-WHAT-IS-IT)

ORIGINS: First sighted in Glastonbury, Connecticut, there have been accounts of this creature throughout the region, though it mostly lives on through the lore and legends of lumberjacks and timbermen who frequent the remote territories where the Glawackus is said to lurk.

DESCRIPTION: Accounts vary as to the description of this creature, some citing it as a large cat, others a large dog, and still others beyond that claiming it is a melding of both feline and canine, though there is some disagreement as to which portions of the animal are which. Popular belief, however, is that the Glawackus is a melding of bear and large cat, either a panther or lion, or perhaps both. By all accounts, the beast is terrifying.

Whatever its composition, this cryptid is estimated to stand between two and two and a half feet at the shoulder and is four feet long, with a two-foot-long tail that some claim is bushy. Its fur ranges from deep black to tawny. Most accounts agree that its other defining features are glowing, ember-like eyes and a horrific screech similar to that of a hyena. Some claim that if you look into the creature's eyes, it will wipe your memory.

LIFE CYCLE: Unknown.

HISTORY: In 1939 multiple sightings of this creature were documented in the Glastonbury area over a period of months. In addition to the eyewitness accounts were reports of howling and blood-curdling screams in the night and a sharp increase in missing pets and mutilated livestock. Dogs that pursued the creature came back injured or not at all.

As the reports continued, the creature was dubbed the Glawackus, some say by a local newspaper editor, others by a Connecticut scientist. All agree that the moniker is a combination of Gla- for Glastonbury, wack- for wacky, and -us to sound suitably scientific.

Many hunting parties set out to track the creature, some caught up in the sensationalism, others with serious intent, well equipped and with hunting dogs. All attempts were unsuccessful, though it became quite the craze with at times as many as two hundred separate hunting parties invading the woods and caves as far as the Berkshires in search of the Glawackus. To this day there are those who advertise the availability of sighting logs to be had. Before the original fervor died down two miles worth of tracks were discovered outside of town, but no other proof was discovered.

In the 1950s a second rash of sightings took place, along with reported incidents similar to those in 1939, this time extending as far north as Granby, but those too died down in a matter of months.

Theories: Some believe that the creature was a puma or large cat escaped from a private collection or zoo, others believe it to be a cat fisher, a species rare in that area but very similar in description to the reported accounts, right down to its terrifying scream. In the end, we can but speculate as the Glawackus continues to elude all efforts to track it down.

Until his decades-long disappearance, JW Harp was known for his trippy underground comic strip *Captain Thetan*, about a seafarer who controls reality for himself and others. This otherworldly character appeared in a dozen issues of the classic rare underground zine *Sandanista Romp*. JW has reemerged thanks largely to eSpec Books' Systema Paradoxa series. In 2023, JW started Skilletfire Studios with comic-book author Scott Eckelaert. Under the Skilletfire Studios mantle, JW has produced the graphic novel *Boylon Heights*, and the *Gimme Five Comics* series. Since its launch, *Gimme Five Comics* has included work by Artyom Topilin, Elena Cerisciola, John L. French, Keith Lansdale, and Joe R. Lansdale with more to come.

JW grew up in the seedy parts of South Carolina, which is all of it. He feels part Canadian and part Costa Rican these days. He lives in North Carolina. Please get in touch with him at jwharp@skilletfire.com.

CAPTURE THE CRYPTIDS!

Cryptid Crate is a monthly subscription box filled with various cryptozoology and paranormal-themed items to wear, display, and collect. Expect a carefully curated box filled with creeptastic pieces from indie makers and artisans pertaining to bigfoot, sasquatch, UFOs, ghosts, and other cryptid and mysterious creatures (apparel, decor, media, etc).

Now Featuring Cryptid Crate Jr.!

http://CryptidCrate.com